Mobile Homes

MOBILE HOMES

NOEL HUDSON

POLESTAR PRESS
WINLAW BC

Mobile Homes

Published by
Polestar Press RR 1 Winlaw BC V0G 2J0 604 226 7670

Acknowledgements
Some of these stories have recently appeared in *The Malahat Review, Capilano Review, Fiddlehead, Wascana Review, Writing* and *Zest*

Canadian Cataloguing in Publication Data
Hudson, Noel, 1956 —
Mobile homes
(Polestar first fiction)
ISBN 0-919591-09-4
I. Title. II. Series.
PS8565.U38M6 1986 C813'.54 C86-091119-5
PR9199.3.H8M6 1986

Cover photo illustration by Jeremy Addington

Mobile Homes was designed and produced by Polestar Press in Winlaw, BC and printed by Hignell Printers in Winnipeg in March 1986.

Note

This is a work of fiction. Names, characters, places and incidents are either the product of the author's imagination or are used fictitiously. Any resemblance to actual events, locales or persons, living or dead, is entirely coincidental.

Mobile Homes is the charter publication in the Polestar First Fiction series. This series will showcase new Canadian writing by presenting the first book of fiction — a novel or collection of short stories — by a Canadian writer.

Mobile Homes

CONTENTS

for Gaye and Wayne
special thanks to Calvin Wharton

MOBILE HOMES

I'M FEELING PRETTY FESTIVE, you understand, being on the escape end of my first week on my new job — forklift operator in a, my god, mobile home factory. "My name is Dixon Haimes and I drive forklift in a mobile home factory." I sound like one of the imposters on *To Tell the Truth*, don't I? Garry Moore asking me, "What is your name, please, and what do you really do?"

This time last week, what I really did was nothing much. Then Monday morning I'm awarded Mr. Most Qualified Applicant. "Dixon Haimes, come on down!" To the mobile home factory out in Cottondale Industrial Park. Chalet Mobile Homes. Wear steel-toed boots and work apparel. That's what he said, "Work apparel."

"That truck unloaded yet?" Chick yells at me.

And I say, "Yellow, Chick," and tip my NAPA cap. "What truck might that be?"

"Rolls aluminum for trim!"

The rin tin tin. "Done and done," I say. Yes, thank you, Chicky. She's bare-bed unloaded in another historical moment, courtesy yours truly, duly unruly.

Chick is the floor manager for the main production building, mister overall overseer. Ever know a man named Chick? Ever know anyone in your whole creeping life named Chick? I at first thought his name was Chet — couldn't be Chick. I asked around and, whatelse, sure enough, Chick he is. Where does a name like that come from, I'd like to know. The joke in Supply is: Chickoslovakia. Chick Selley. Like a little missile. Heavyish man, tapered at the head. He doesn't move much, but when he does he sort of fires himself at you.

Boom Chick-a-licka-licka! Boom Chick-a-licka-licka! I wanna take you higher!

We're probably off on the wrong foot. I've only been here a week, right, and thus far Chick has caught me taking a pause behind Finishing, leaving a refrigerator in the delivery lane (I was coming right back for it), dropping a pallet of roofing shingles because I picked them up off-center and was too busy to put them down and try again, and, well, trying to lift a corner of the main production building (there was a gap wide enough to get my forks underneath — I don't know, just late-in-the-day curiosity). It's not like I do this kind of thing all the time; it's just that I seem to be on Chick the Missile's radar tracking system.

If you've never worked in a mobile home factory yourself, you have missed something. Though I know not exactly what. It generally looks to me like we're just a bunch of dumb animals making our own cages. Cranking out the product. Go-go gophers. *Production time, assembly line, widgets per minute, and ten beats nine. Say push.*

Makin' mo' mo' mobile homes.

If you're, say, a carpenter or a bricklayer, and you're putting up a house on a piece of land, watching it slowly take shape, become part of a neighbourhood, a community, then you must really feel like you're making a house, imagine a family living in it. But when you crawl into a steel building the size of a shopping mall, with no natural light, at five fifty-nine a.m., and you start stapling and/or power-screwing parts to be stapled and/or power-screwed to other parts, to be wrapped in aluminum and trailered out the door to Finishing in a great blinding blast of outside light, you don't get the true sense of what you're making. You don't get any sense whatsoever. About half the employees here, I'm told, live in mobile homes themselves, and I swear none of them makes the connection.

"*Mo*billy homes," a guy on the TV commercials calls them.

Iggy Pop, foremost innovator of rock'n'roll, when asked by *The New Music* why he was so strange, rambunctious and spastic during the performance of his songs, said, "I grew up in a trailer house." That covered it. The interviewer didn't ask for more. He knew what Pop was saying, and I do too. I did some time in one of these things myself, when I was eight and nine and my parents, ever modern, bought the "Homes of the Future" line. Every room was like your spare bathroom, all squeezed to fit, a house squeezed into a Velveeta cheese box. We had two dogs, Trixie and Vodka, and both of them went crazy and started biting people — us included. None of our dogs did that before or after the mobile home. I think Iggy Pop, when he one day writes his rock autobiography, should title it *I Grew Up in a Trailer House.* I'd buy it.

These are mobile homes not trailer houses, let there be no mistake. Chick already fined me a quarter for calling them trailer houses. It's like when I drove forklift in a paper plant that made cardboard boxes, and we were supposed to call them corrugated paper products. Another part of the plant made toilet paper. What were they supposed to say? Rolled tissue? Try it with a British accent.

See you later, corrugator. In a while, Gomer Pyle. At the paper plant we called the employees who suffered acute failure-to-think-fast gomers. There are some dues-paying gomers here too.

Chick again. I'm unloading a stack of two-by-fours at one of the saw stations, these to be cut for wall studs, when what to my wandering eyes should appear. Chick. From nowhere. Glaring, as is his usual expression. I salute.

"How we holding for Boutique?" he wants to know, like I'm expected to have all the bathroom panelling patterns memorized and keep a running-brain inventory.

"Two bundles," I say. I have no idea.

"Potpourri?"

"We're out."

"Fancy Florentine?"

"Five bundles." I have worked enough places to know what they want is an answer, right or not.

Chick jots on his clipboard, which is strung around his little missile neck on a shoelace. He dismisses me, but he's gone before I am. I don't know how he does it. Zip. *Here a Chick, there a Chick, everywhere a Chick-Chick.*

Bebop amoeba, she's my baby. Bebop amoeba, I don't mean maybe.

I idle a while, let some more Friday afternoon slip by, keep a look out for this Debbie I have my eye on. She's a sweeper, keeps the aisles clear of mobile home debris. Debbie with the pale green eyes and equally charming thighs. It was a surprise to me to discover she worked here. I met her once before, months ago. I was a couple of beers into an Australian movie about a boy and his pelican when she knocked. It turned out she was pounding down doors on a donation drive for money to send local hemophiliac kids to medically-supervised summer camp, but I didn't know that.

"Sir," she said to me, "I'll bet like most people you think only royal Russian children like young Czarevitch Alexander, son of Czar Nicholas and Czarina Alexandra, get hemophilia. Well, of course, that's not factual."

If she was asking me to give blood, then I was ready for her. I was enrolled in a regular blood donation program. I thought I could put a fast damper on this and get back to Storm Boy and his pelican. She looked tasty, but what are you going to say to hustle a woman on a hemophilia drive?

"I give blood," I said.

"That's extremely thoughtful," she replied, taking a seat.

I strode over and turned down the volume on the television, being polite, but first listening to a few lines of dialogue to keep track of plot development. Several men in a boat were caught in a severe storm right offshore from where Storm Boy and his fisherman father lived in their remote and humble shack. The boat's sails were torn and the engine was kaput. High waves and helplessness. The boy's aborigine friend saw the boat, the men aboard, and ran to tell Storm Boy.

"Hemophiliacs' blood lacks the essential clotting ingredient you and I take for granted," she said. Then some more about missing factor infusions, famous hemophiliacs, regular ones living careful lives right here in our city, and so on.

I was still waiting for her to ask for my blood, to get to the point. I could tell this was a crucial scene in the movie. Storm scenes are always crucial. She had a nice voice.

"Sometimes it's a light blow to the head that can cause internal bleeding in the brain or spinal cord. Every time something like this happens in a hemophiliac's life, he or she is in danger of dying," she said. Then, "They just gave that pelican a tow rope. And he flew it out to the men in that boat. That pelican saved those people!"

She put hemophilia on hold and we watched the end of the movie together. She apologized to me for getting off the topic, but it had been a long day. She had already canvassed a whole other apartment building that evening. We cried together when the hunters shot the pelican, and when the aborigine took Storm Boy to the pelican's burial site, but we cried the most when the music swelled and the Australian sky filled with pelicans. Her wet green and gold-flecked eyes. She explained the hemophiliac summer camp over a glass of iced tea, and I wrote her a cheque for five dollars — not having gainful employment then.

I saw her sweeping here my first day and thought: divine

providence. She's been playing shy, though. Teaser.

I see her down by Cabinets. "Hel-lo, Debbie," I call through the assembling din.

She looks up, gives a little wave. I got time.

"You bought a plot?" a guy asks me, carrying a sink to the home in second position.

Thet-thet-thet-thet. There's a staplegun attack coming from Floors. These are real blitzkriegs. You get docked a half-day's pay and put on probation — under the eye of Chick — if you're caught shooting at anything except a piece of mobile home. I'm inside the rear of the building, delivering particle board. Particle board — sounds atomic, doesn't it? Putting down a floor at the molecular level. Sounds ten to the tenth power more interesting than what it actually is, which is wood chips compressed into sheets the size and shape of plywood. They don't even use the lowest grade plywood in these units. Wood chips, like you'd toss on the floor of a gerbil cage. Compress the stuff and these gomers construct the floor of your mobile home with it.

Three guys from Floors crew fire bursts of inch-long staples at the rolls of pink fiberglass insulation stacked on planks above the Interior Walls station. The staples tear through the paper holding the rolls together and the pink erupts, grows, unrolls, comes crashing down on the head of Odis "The Wall" Gauger. Odis emerges, itching pink, seeing red, flinging blocks of wood into Floors section. The blocks skip across the particle board, missing the three gunners, who yell at him. "Hey, Odis my man, what gives?" "Damn, I almost lost an eye there, Wall!" "Something disturbing you, Odis? Is this friendly? What is this all about, son?" It's about these fools being bored out of their trees and it being just an hour to quitting time.

Odis is big enough to carry his finished product — an entire wall — to the assembly line and hold it steady for five minutes while lesser mortals nail it in place. He works alone at his station, quietly, but now screams, "Die, Floor People! Eat carp and die!" He gives up on the wood blocks and fires his own staplegun, shoots a streak high along the rear wall of the building, raising tiny dark clouds of factory dust and sprayed-on swamp-green wall foam, which float and dissipate over the Floor People like sinister pollutants in chemical warfare. Gagging, coughing, one of the original snipers fires another round above Odis, this time managing to puncture the air hose supplying Odis's gun. There is the flat quack of a staplegun sucking for compression, and the Floor People make the woowoo woowoo howler monkey cries used to get plant attention. Then, "Odis! Odis! Odis! Odis!"

Chick is up on the skywalk at the front of the building with Norbert, the plant manager. He's looking this direction, but there's a lot to look at at this end of the line. He rubs his forehead and turns to peer into the roofless home directly below him. There is so much noise, I'm almost certain he can't hear the Floor People chant. Odis throws his staplegun aside, hammers on his wall with a claw hammer, and carries it to the line.

Maintenance Mike, a former communications technician in Nam, hears the quacking and arrives to fix the air hose. I stick around because I'll have to raise him up on my forks to patch the puncture. Mike likes to talk Nam — which I don't mind listening to, but don't quite comprehend either. I think maybe he took some shrapnel; I have an uncle talks the same way about WWII.

"... from Cam Lo, Route Nine into Khe Sanh, bad-ass walk," says Mike, smearing a clear substance on the hose hole.

One of the Floors gomers comes over to explain to Mike how I raised my forks nine feet up and, backing off and lunging forward repeatedly, stabbed at the hose until it popped.

"Sure shit, George," I say. I call everyone on Floors George. There are eight of them.

"...UPI boys sitting pretty in the DMZ, fat photo opportunity, click-click, some hometown heroes, me bap-bap-bap-headed with the din of AK-47s way to hell elsewhere. Like photo that if you U-P-I dare..."

Odis returns to start another wall, but first gives my vertical-lift lever a slap, and Mike a downward jolt.

"Dang, dang, got to get to Danang."

"He was never in Nam," Odis tells me confidentially.

"War Zone C, above Cu Chi," says Mike. "Cong men, Cong women, Cong kids — even the wildfowl was Cong."

"Lived next to me the whole time," says Odis. "Watched it on his mother's color Quasar." Odis is nodding, agreeing with himself.

Debbie sweeps her debris up the aisle between Floors and Interior Walls, toward us, looking casual as can be, and I lean coolly back in my forklift seat, Maintenance Mike high overhead. I hike a suggestive eyebrow.

"Hi, Odis," she says. I know she's teasing me.

"Hi, Deb," he says, working madly with his hammer to keep up, fighting downtime. "Just sweep that garbage over there. Floor People eat that."

"I bought me a pelican," I say, give her a wink. "Want to come by and see him?"

She gives my outstretched leg a slow brush with her broom, not looking me in the eye. Casual, causal.

"Tet Offensive," says Mike. "Two hundred grunts."

He's patched the air hose and motions for me to bring him down. On the ground, he gives me a sloppy white soul shake and jogs off to repair something else.

"Think I'll call him Storm Bird," I say.

My last girlfriend, Robin, lived in a mobile home park with her father. The park was set up in a racetrack oval, with homes running down either side and a row down the center island. I'd go out to pick her up after dark, see the three lines of mobile homes gleaming in the full moonlight, looking not unlike spaceships lined up awaiting the Leader's signal, prepared to launch right off the planet at a moment's notice, singly or in squadrons, or the entire park complete. It was like I could leave, return in half an hour, and the park would be empty, just disappearing lines of glittering mobile homes moving toward the moon, headed for deep space. That's what I liked to think.

But these homes had undergone standard procedure demobilization. They'd been strapped down against high winds, their wheels and tires removed, their axles blocked up on cinder blocks. The one's in Robin's section were skirted — some with stained wood, some with vinyl or aluminum siding, usually color-coordinated with the home itself. The residents therein were saying: We are not transients, migrant laborers or fly-by-nighters; we are not mobile; we are no different than people who live in real houses.

Mobile home parks have their own neighborhoods, and whenever someone leaves there is usually a shuffle, residents trying to get a better spot. Robin and her father moved seven times. In the same mobile home park. When I was seeing her, they were in one of the better sections, where cube-shaped green aluminum tool sheds were mandatory. And lawn ornaments. Her dad had a bright red knee-high toadstool and some blue dwarves. Their home was a Pawnee Presidential, white with mustard trim.

I didn't meet her father for the longest time. "Dad's at one of his gun club meetings," she'd always say when I'd pick her up. This went on for the longest time. And I became somewhat uneasy with the knowledge that her father was meeting almost nightly to talk with likeminds about guns: how to care for them, how to put them to good use.

One night she and I were getting excited, right there in her old man's mobile home, when his pickup pulled into the drive. *Close Encounters* was on the tube, so we got up off the floor and started talking animatedly about it. We waited for him to charge in. Waited and waited. I was wondering if it really was him.

"It's him," she said. "He does this. Keep talking."

"The special effects are what make it happen for me," I said. "And the part where they come for the woman's kid."

"Yes," she said, craning her neck to see out the window. "The way they unscrew the floor vents and you think they're coming right in."

And then he was in. In. Her father was inside with us. I didn't even see the door open. He was just there. People often appear like that before me, maybe I should pay closer attention.

"Who's he?" her father asked.

"Daddy, this is Dixon Haimes."

"Okay," he said.

I thought, He's not going to let me off this easy.

"You two want pizza?" He lifted the lid off a large Mino's Greco-Roman Pizza box. Shrimp and onion.

I'd expected him to be carrying a rifle or two. I don't know why I assumed gun club members took their guns with them to meetings.

We passed the pizza and he plopped down between us on the couch. "Whatcha watchin'?"

"*Close Encounters*."

"That the one where the guy makes the mud mountain in his living room because the aliens put that fixation in his brain?"

"That's the one, Dad. You've seen it."

"I like that one," he said, chewing.

"He likes aliens," she said.

"Two of you dating, or this it?"

"We're dating. I'm thinking of keeping him, what do you think?"

He didn't reply, just opened his full mouth at her. Robin flicked a shrimp off his pizza and it stuck to his face. He still didn't say anything. We watched the mother ship land.

Finally, he asked, "When's he leave?"

"Depends," she said, "on how long you stay out here being parental."

"Uh-huh. The guy goes with the aliens in the end, right?"

"Right. I told you, you've seen it."

"Well then," he said, exchanged some nonverbal father-daughter business and shuffled down the hall to his bedroom.

It was about thirty seconds after the door closed that I heard *sha-shunk* the shift of a rifle bolt, and I was outta there.

Outside — it was after midnight — there was a tractor moving a home over from one lot to the next.

"Dong!" the carpetcutter hollers from the far side of Floors.

Oh, my dong is ten feet long. Beat that, Godzilla! Beat that, King Kong.

The dong is a ten-foot steel pole which attaches to the forklift and enables me to spear the core tubes of carpet and linoleum rolls. I used one at the paper plant for bulk rolls of paper. I have to lift down the rolls of floor covering needed for the home in Floors position. There are about forty assorted rolls on the rack.

"New guy," says Carpetcutter, greeting me.

"Carpetcutter."

We clip the dong on between the forks. It's heavy. I dong him down the required roll of linoleum, and listen while he cuts. He wants to get into recreational vehicles.

"Work isn't the thing anymore," he says. "Work is on its way out. The future is leisure time. With advanced technology in the workplace, greatly increased productivity and decreased man-hours, flex-time, job sharing, leaves of absence, people are about to be drowned in leisure time. People are going to be bored. Boredom is the next wave, and recreation is the only antidote. And by recreation I don't mean sport, I don't mean activity and perspiration. I mean driving around looking at things. I'm studying the construction process here at the hands-on level and getting paid for it! Three years' time, I'm not kidding, I'll have my own RV factory, manufacturing around the clock to keep up with raging demand. I already see the essential modifications, the corners to be cut, the way to provide a luxury look through inexpensive structural enhancement. I can make a recreational vehicle anybody can afford — half the price the cheapest one goes for today! I'm finished with this. What I need is a roll of Spanish Pimiento. I've got living room and hall to cut for an Arapaho Modern."

Debbie shows up with a carpetcutting tool she found in her sweepings.

"How's she going'?" I say.

"Glad it's about over," she says. "My legs're about to give out."

I study her legs. "Want a lift somewhere?" I move over on the seat, make room.

"Get real," she says, looking down the aisles.

"Want to go for a drive after work, then?"

Chick. He must use a transporter beam.

"You think you could finish out the day?" he asks, "Would that be inconvenient, Dixon? You think you could restock panelling for Finishing? You think, maybe?"

Carpetcutter grimaces behind the Chickadee and gives me the thumb to vamoose.

I'm looking at about five minutes remaining. I get up top speed, come flying blindly around the corner of the main building, not knowing what will be there — I used to do this at the paper plant — *a gas-gas-gas*, zinging, leaning with it, spine tingling, like my spinal fluid's gone effervescent, pure rush. I take a wide turn to compensate for the forklift's small wheelbase, *Go, Johnny, Go, Go*, give the horn a half-hearted beep, see the runway's cleared for landing. I wind it down, drop my forks and slide them under a pallet of sinks I was supposed to deliver to Bathrooms over an hour ago, but it will wait for Monday. Then I see goddamn Chick. Again! Standing outside

Supply Room door, staring at me and fanning his neck with his clipboard. And I know he saw the complete lame cheap-thrill stunt. I figure I got me a missile crisis. I lift the sinks and turn around, planning to rush them inside, maybe work a few minutes overtime, but he's gone again.

The buzzer sounds. I leave the forklift parked where it is and, thinking I'll dodge the Chick, I don't go back inside. I run around front, shoulder through the worker bees to punch out — and there's a note clipped to my time-card. "I want you to stop by tonight between 7-7:30. We should have a talk." Chick's home address is on the back.

No problem. I was looking for a job when I found this one.

Chick's house is a brick ranch-style on West Elm. There is a marble bird bath on the front lawn, with birds actually using it. I don't park in the driveway, choosing the street instead, public property, not crossing the moat.

He opens the door before I can even ring the bell. I think about just saying, "I quit, okay?" and getting out of there, but I see Debbie sitting in a recliner in the living room and figure she's not there collecting for hemophilia, but what did she do, really? She was returning a tool, that's all.

"Hi," she says meekly.

I smile and roll my shoulders inside my jacket.

"You like a drink, Dixon?" Chick says.

"I don't believe I will, thank you."

Chick takes me on a tour of the house. He did all the cabinet-work himself, he tells me, and I recognize the lower kitchen cupboards as mobile home stock from the factory — the good stuff, but not real wood. I recognize a couple of carpet patterns too. He's being Mr. Hospitality, and I'm just tagging along behind two steps, agreeing and making throat noises. There is a pool table in the basement, and he asks if I play. Yes, some. "It's a soothing game, isn't it?" he asks.

On the way up the stairs I glance out the basement window

and see a two-bedroom Estate Vista Palatial parked in the backyard. It's blocked up and skirted nicely. There is a bird bath in the front of it, too. "Debbie's mom and dad," Chick says, standing at the top of the stairs.

I wait for him to finish. What is it, he's phoning employees' parents now?

"They were reluctant, but I told them, 'Why do you want to pay for a lot?' Won't be long until her dad's retiring and they'll be on fixed income. Only makes sense. We've got this huge big yard and no bylaws against us. 'Park it here, and we'll be sure to come to dinner once a week,' I said. Works out fine."

We go into the living room, where Debbie is nibbling from a fruit and cheese plate, sit down, Chick next to her.

"I think it's great you want to be friends with my wife," he says, "but I think, in the context of the workplace, you know, at the factory, a businesslike attitude is appropriate, don't you?"

My wife, he says! "Most assuredly," I say, never having used that phrase before, wondering on hearing it blurted where the hell it came from. Wife. I give Chick a close going over. He's maybe not as old as I originally placed him, but he still has fifteen years on Debbie. *Ah, my little Chickadee!* This is so good, I don't even care, don't even feel like I've lost out. *... even the wildfowl was Cong*. Hot damn. And mom and dad parked out back in a mobile home!

"I'm glad we cleared this matter up, Dixon. I thought it might be best to bring it up outside the factory, as it is very nearly a personal issue, you understand. I don't know. It was a close call, and I don't like to come down too hard on a guy his first week. It's not my nature and it's not good management."

"Thank you," I say, the festivity rising in me again. "I appreciate it."

I have that drink and listen to Chick go on about my basic conscientious nature and how he can see I'll level out in the weeks ahead and be a benefit to the plant. Debbie relaxes a bit and talks about the hemophiliac summer camp, about hating her sweeping job but being in line for the next opening on the line. Chick guarantees it. She rubs his missile back while he reviews production statistics, gives me the total picture. We play pool for pocket change. We play Yahtzee and eat Penguin cookies in the Estate Vista Palatial with Chick's in-laws. I feel like family. I'm rolling the dice for a large straight when it hails like a hundred zombies coming down on us with ball-peen hammers, hails like all hell, marble-size, golf ball-size, smashes every window in the place and traps us for almost an hour in that tin can trailer house mobile home, immobilized, the din of AK-47s, me bap-bap-bap-headed, and each of us looking like who's going to bite who first.

BUFFALO

BUFFALOATING. It was out there on the pond like a humped-up cabin rug — but slick shiny haired, as though the entire beast had been done over with boot polish. The grey tongue floated in the water, and every few seconds the head dunked, then popped up again eyefirst. I chucked a rock, a dead-on shot. Nothing. One of Boog's black bass spooked nearby, but the rock splotted off hair island without stirring it the least. I was cutting school, doing the free man hookey, and this looked like the agenda.

Boog drove over the rise and across the pasture toward the pond in his fence-examining vehicle, a turquoise '73 Mercury Marquis. I motioned him over, though he was coming anyway, and he flashed his headlights.

"Now look what you done," said Boog, rolling his no-hips off the brocade seat.

"I just found it. How long's it been out here?"

"Since yesterday noon, at least."

"Was it dead then?"

"Appeared so."

Boog was flapping in the breeze. He had on his Wrangler SuperBells, widening to the earth like rocket bottoms, and one of his Romeo-sleeved shirts, complete with hang-gliding collar, the whole outfit blue and frayed and vintage almost before I was born. *Mod Squad* clothes, as can only be seen on syndicated reruns and Boog. He looked nothing like a rancher, and certainly not a buffalo keeper.

''Carnoe'll be here presently,'' he said.

Carnoe was the renderer from Hooverton. I had his pencil.

CARNOE RENDERING COMPANY
TALLOW — FAT — GREASE — BONES
985-6351
"EAT MORE MEAT"

He was by our place to pick up a horse last year. The nimble steed had danced herself into a disker, then panicked. Double lame. Bye bye, Roni.

''Can't they swim?'' I asked Boog.

The buffalo's head was underwater and one silvery horn protruded like a shark's fin. Up popped the eye.

''It's Rooter,'' said Boog. ''One of the originals. They can swim, but they're not real efficient. And he was old.''

''He drowned?''

Boog said, ''Heart attack maybe. Swum himself out there and didn't have it to swim back. Beats me. *Why* he swum out there is a question for you. Might've thought he saw something. I think they hallucinate sometimes — heat mirages or just things from their imagination — standing out here in this heat, under all that head of fur.''

We sat on the hood of Boog's car, our backs against the windshield, watching the buffaloat. I told him my word and he grinned, but I doubt I picked the best time. Boog was tied in to some government preservation program. The more buffalo he could produce, the more they paid him. He just had to keep them alive and reproducing. So he was usually talking estrus and cervical dilation. Unfortunately, he'd only had one calf the year before and it was a bull. Little thing reminded me of a wildebeest on one of those Sunday-afternoon wild Africa shows.

''I guess he's more or less replaced by the new guy,'' said

Boog, "but that's all. I'm not having much luck with these animals. I think Gigi's got a virus."

Gigi was a two-year-old buffalo cow with big chocolate eyes. Boog's girlfriend, Tammy, one time painted Gigi's hooves red, and even tried to put lipstick on her. But Gigi butted Tammy in the chest and knocked the wind out of her. The red paint on the hooves lasted a long time. Boog was mad because government Ag people came out every so often unannounced to look over the herd. Boog ordered Tammy to remove the paint, but she machine-gunned her shirt snaps and showed him her bruise, etcetera, and so, as you can imagine, got out of it. I was on-site for the display, watching Boog cover her amples with his hands while telling me to go fish. Tammy smiled at me like we were sharing a secret. And no one got around to taking the paint off Gigi, or maybe she wouldn't allow it — she got extra attention because she was easy to spot.

Boog had gone contemplative, staring sullenly beyond the bass pond. Coming out of it, he said, "What the hell was he doing? Damn you, Rooter, you flea-bite old scout!" And he whapped the Mercury's antenna, made it whip audible circles.

"How do they float?" I asked.

Boog kicked at the sky in what seemed to be an involuntary spasm, spit downwind, listened to me not repeat the question, and finally answered, "Fat floats. And the gas and air inside them, I suppose. Hell, I don't know. Ask Carnoe when he gets here. I'm not the one to ask. Carnoe can tell you whatever you want to know."

"Sorry."

"The thing is," said Boog, "I have three less now than when I started. I couldn't give them much more attention. I'm all for the long-term, but I spend most of my time coddling buffalo when I should be tending to other things. Still, I mean, you get up in the morning, walk outside, look at the cattle, look at the buffalo, and you know immediately where your priority should lie. There is a responsibility to history. And, my god, it should be simple enough to repopulate a herd. But every damned year it's fertility problems, false pregnancies, miscarriages, virus, disease, coyotes, week-long blizzards — now Rooter."

Boog whapped the antenna again.

Carnoe showed up minutes later in his winch truck. CARNOE RENDERING COMPANY, it said on the side, SYMPATHETIC PROFESSIONAL RENDERING – AS SEEN ON TV.

I didn't remember him being so short. He was about my height, but weighed more than Boog and I put together, maybe twice. He was round, solid, stern-looking, and he sported full white General Ambrose E. Burnside sideburns.

"That's the saddest sight of my week," Carnoe said sincerely, clapping Boog on the knee. "Yes, it is."

Boog and I slid off the car and walked with him down to the edge of the pond. We scoped out the Rooter situation for a couple of minutes, during which time a bass darted up and nipped at the dead grey tongue.

"We'd better haul him out before the fish eat him," said Carnoe. He turned to me and added, "There are fish in this world that could consume that animal in the time it took you to say 'Jack Sprat would eat no fat.'"

Piranha, I thought. But I didn't say. I didn't want to be wrong. He eyed me and waited, inviting me to guess incorrectly. I knew that was what he was doing.

"I've heard that," I said, feeling I had to reply before I could move.

"What'd you hear?" he asked in his same matter-of-fact face.

Boog called him away. The renderer said, "I like you, kid. You're okay," and jabbed me in the stomach with his thumb.

Carnoe backed his truck down to the pond while Boog got out of his clothes. He cranked out plenty of slack for the chain cradle, and Boog and I half-swung half-tossed it in Rooter's general direction. It sunk immediately. Carnoe stripped too, and he and Boog, odd bodies in their undershorts, waded out into the pond. Boog dipped under and retrieved the chain cradle, and the two of them swam it to the buffalo. They wrestled quite some time getting it fastened properly, and there were moments when the man-manipulated animal seemed to come alive again, air bubbles rushing from its mouth and nostrils, wooly head lolling like he was just playing dead. Bluffaloating. The two men spoke in hushed voices against the sides of the sopped carcass — paid their respects.

They swam to shore and dragged themselves onto the grass, hitched their wet shorts up and shook in the early afternoon sun. Carnoe banged a lever on the side of his truck and the chain commenced reeling with a sorrowful moan. Rooter glided through the dark green pond water. Carnoe and Boog stood beside me in reverent silence, dripping, wet cotton clinging to their butts. They looked sad. They looked like the fall of Rome.

"Might save the hide for you, though I wouldn't promise," said Carnoe, once Rooter was on dry land.

The winch continued to raise the buffalo until he shut it off. Rooter hung limply in the chain cradle while Boog pried his mouth open, peering inside past the thick obstructing tongue.

"No need," said Boog. "I need live animals. I don't need hide, horns, innards, mounted heads, or anything else *but* the live animal."

"What are you looking for?" I asked.

"I don't know," he replied, and let the heavy head drop.

Carnoe hit the lever again and the winch towed Rooter onto the back of the truck. Water flowed from the body and pooled around it. Behind Rooter, I could see a dead cow, a polled Hereford.

"You truant?" asked Boog.

"Field trip," I said. He knew.

"Well, I'm following Carnoe over to Hooverton. You can stay and fish if you want to."

I pictured the bass chewing Rooter's dead tongue.

"No thanks," I said, without suggesting another option, just shrugging and fidgeting.

"Get in and I'll field trip you over to Hoover," said Carnoe, wiping his sideburns down his neck to wring out the remaining water.

I looked to Boog, who had his wet shorts off and was crawling into his bellbottoms.

"I'll bring you home," he said.

Stick to the agenda. I had never been to Hooverton, and I had never been involved in the transport of a drowned buffalo. I got into the cab of the rendering truck.

"You sure you don't want to ride in back, keep an eye on the merchandise?" Carnoe asked.

We tuned in to K-Country radio and bumped back across the pasture. Boog shot by us in his Marquis, going ahead to open the gate.

Pulling onto the road, Carnoe said, "Now you see anything dead, you be sure to point it out to me."

I was almost certain he was kidding.

"You heard about them cows that had their hearts and sex organs removed, didn't you?" Carnoe asked. "You did hear about that?"

The seats in the truck's cab gave off a strangely sweet odor, overpowering the half-foot-high pine tree air freshener on the dashboard.

I had already disappointed Carnoe by not having heard about the train derailment outside Milliard that near-fatally endangered hundreds when a large tank-car filled with chlordane almost toppled and burst. It had been held upright by a jack-knifed boxcar containing crates of Diamond and Ruby Miracle Crucifixes, each tiny crucifix having a sealed vault located in its hollowed-out back. In the vaults, according to Carnoe, were earth from the holy site of Jesus's birth in Bethlehem and authentic water from Lourdes. These combined in some sort of miracle mud. And I hadn't heard about the retired janitor whose locust tree hissed and rattled at him whenever he stepped out of his house, even on totally calm days. But I had heard about the cows with their sex organs mysteriously removed.

"Of course I heard," I said.

"What'd you hear?"

My mind raced to think of something not too stupid or kid-like to say, and I had only heard that it happened and that was all, but Carnoe decided not to wait.

"I was the one called in to haul them away," he said. "I'll bet you didn't know that. I was right there, bodyside. Fetching a cow is one of the worst things anyway, but *four* of them, all mutilated. Let that settle for a minute. A horse isn't bad. A horse these days is a pleasure animal, a pet. If you lose a horse, you lose pleasure is all. But a cow, you understand, is a farmer's livelihood. I hate being called for a cow, because I know its effect. People have great respect for their cattle. The health of their cattle is the health of their farm. There's genuine respect. They don't worship them like Indians, mind you. East Indians. India Indians. You've heard of sacred cows. I've seen pictures of cows strolling down city sidewalks like bankers. India is cow Shangri-la. Cows are on par with people — maybe higher status than some people. You've heard it said, 'as useless as an abattoir in India'? Cows are sacred, because to Indians they are incarnations. East Indians, not our native Indians, which you would think would be West Indians but aren't. West Indians live in the West Indies. Our Indians aren't even Indians, if you can believe it! It was Christopher Columbus who called them Indians. They teach you that in school?"

"We had some Columbus," I said, "and some Magellan, some de Gama, some Vespucci."

"These organless cows were on a place over near Mingo,

just north of where the deodorant plant used to be.''

A corridor of hybrid commercial sunflowers crowded the two-lane highway, their bright yellow heads following the imperceptible movement of the sun, each head almost a foot in diameter. The sunflower heads were level with the truck's windows. We were deep in a forest of sunflowers.

Carnoe gave me a look sober as a Baptist usher.

''No man cut those organs out,'' he said. ''I can tell you that much. The cuts were completely unknifelike and done in a curious pattern, for no apparent reason. Pencil-line narrow burn marks. Singed hair and hide. Neat as you please. They're calling it mutilation, but there's a better word somewhere, considering the way it was done. Clay Willoughby's son, Feryll, helped me out up there, he can attest to what I'm saying. He was one of the head honchos at the deodorant plant, right up until it blew. That was a year ago March, I believe. They say it was the extra anti-wetness ingredient that was primarily responsible, a chemical imbalance, a chain reaction, the whole horrid mess self-combusting to hell. Feryll was the one who smelled it coming and got everyone out in time. Except the orange-haired quality control woman from Mattoon. I know your people aren't from the Mattoon area, so I don't mind saying that Mattoonites are a high-brow inbred bunch. The mayor's in-laws, all of them. This one insisted on increasing the extra anti-wetness ingredient, ran crazy, dumping beakers full into the deodorants vats, which not long later took off the roof, a few eyebrows, her orange hair, kicked out a sonic boom of aerosol can explosions, and shut the plant down for good. This was bootleg deodorant, you understand, the real aerosol spray stuff they banned in '78 on the claim that the propellant molecules were eating up the ozone. You know the ozone? It's like a protective layer around the earth, filtering out harmful-to-human rays. But people like their aerosol. The blow-up put nine people out of work, including Feryll Willoughby. A real rabbit punch to the Mingo economy.

The place may not survive it. Plus, Mingo people are forced to spend their lives alternately sunburned and snowblind as a result of the lost ozone directly above their town. There should've been some government aid money, but they couldn't tell anyone, you see. It was their secret, signed and sealed. But to this day not a one of them sweats, nor will they ever. You've never seen a fresher-looking town of people."

He gave me time for retort, but what? I hadn't been there, and I sensed he was counting on that, ready to deliver his first-hand account to a know-nothing kid, perched to swoop.

I could see Boog driving behind us in the door mirror. He had his left boot on the dashboard and was slumped down, slapping time on his headrest. From here, it looked like he was slapping the back of his head. He had three main bands he listened to: Black Sabbath, Grateful Dead, and Ten Years After. Riding in Boog's car was *the* bass experience — high-power quad system, pre-equalizer, blown tweeters and concert woofers. Carnoe and I sat through a festival of old Roger Miller hits: "King of the Road," "England Swings (Like A Pendulum Do)," "You Can't Rollerskate (In A Buffalo Herd)," "Dang Me (You Oughta Take A Rope And Hang Me)." My eyes drifted from the renderer's pulpy, sideburn-enhanced face, to the blurry passing of giant sunflowers, to Boog, in the mirror, pounding his headrest, and back again. On the road to Hooverton. And I realized Carnoe had started without me.

"I wouldn't choose to live among them," he said. "Not in a million years, I wouldn't. Most Mingo people are Joe's Witnesses. Not Feryll, none of the Willoughbys. And there are a couple of other families I can testify aren't. But most, you understand, are Joe's. Not so much the farmers and ranchers, but the Mingo townspeople, dry as they are. How many worked in the deodorant plant, I couldn't say. To be honest, I don't recall if deodorant usage is against their beliefs. Perfume is, of course, and aftershave lotion, dancing, motion pictures, and television. The ones working in the plant didn't have to use the deodorant, I suppose, just make it. I don't know what the ruling on that would be. They had it used on them in the end though, didn't they? Keep them composed down at the Kingdom Hall. Let's just say they'd outnumber you thirty to one in Mingo. And they don't drive much, so they do most of their witnessing in town limits. And not to each other, you can bet. About how many times a day do you reckon a nonJoe's would hear 'We're just going around talking to people today about something that's on most everybody's mind. Do you think the world is in a troubled state?'? Your only safe answer being 'No. I think the world is a sweet field of clover.' The trick is to get you agreeing with them, all of you smiling and agreeing, then they migrate microscopically into religion, and before you know it they're saying 'Christ is among us,' and you're still answering 'That's sure true.' He may well be among us, but he's not in Mingo, I'll tell you that. He's not in the one spot on earth without an ozone. All the Mingo Joe's are waiting around, hoping for the absolute worst, so that Jesus will make Himself known to them. That's their principle belief. Things will get out of hand, a battle will line up between Joe's Witnesses and all the nations and organized religions of the world, and Jesus will intervene on the Joe's behalf, hurling natural disasters and plagues, causing the death of billions, and leaving a peaceful sin-free earth populated by Joe's chosen. This why they loved the cow mutilations so much."

We emerged from the sunflower forest onto a vast landscape of wheat, corn, milo and sugar beets; fallow fields, cow pastures and scrublands; grids; acres, hectares, square kilometres, square miles, sections, half-sections, quarter-sections; county roads, family farms and failing windbreaks. The flat of the land. Carnoe pointed out Hooverton, twelve miles ahead, and scattered towns beyond.

"That's the main reason I had Feryll give me a hand. I needed somebody to keep the Joe's Witnesses at a distance. The entire flock turned out — and most of them walked all the way from town. They circled the four dead cows and pointed fingers. 'It is a symbolic act,' they said. 'It is His will. It is His warning. The heart and sexual organs, yes.' And even I could see that no *man* had done the cutting, which didn't settle my stomach, staring at those perfect burn-cut incisions and having a flock of Joe's pointing and praising." Carnoe shuddered.

Ten miles out, we hit a series of potholes and new asphalt-patch welts, bringing both of us off the seat and slamming the animals around in the back of the truck. Carnoe cursed, swerved maniacally. Bodies bounced and groaned, theirs and ours, the truck itself. Out of it, Carnoe picked up his pace.

"They huddled around the mutilated cows, just as close as Feryll would let them get, poking at the overly curious with a shovel handle. They looked from the cows to me, to the cows, huddled together blank-faced, agreeing with each other whatever was said, saying 'It is written,' giving me the blue willies, a handful of them gazing off into the ozoneless north-of-Mingo sky, expressionless. It was obvious to them."

Boog had disappeared from my mirror. The turquoise Mercury was no longer behind us.

"Now I know," continued Carnoe. "It is obvious to me. Many things are now obvious to me. The Joe's were right to be staring up at the sky, but wrong as can be in what they were thinking. How long's a light year? You get that in school?"

"Elementary geometry," I replied, "square roots."

"I didn't think so," said Carnoe, his suspicion confirmed. "Then you can't begin to figure four hundred and thirty-two million light years, can you? You have no grasp of that."

"What's it in miles? I can get it if you give me some numbers. What's a light year come to in miles?"

"You'd need knowledge beyond numbers to comprehend a light year," he said. His voice became more darkly somber, became monochromatic. "You heard about the UFO sightings west of Hooverton, didn't you? Newspapers were full of it, no way you could've missed it. Last Friday night, between nine and quarter to eleven. One man said they looked like glowing pipe tobacco cans — which is about as uneducated an opinion as you'd hope to find. He claimed they hovered over his house, probing the yard with sensor beams at irregular intervals, then vanished and reappeared in another part of the sky. That's what he called them, 'sensor beams,' And he got that part right, bless him."

"Bullshit," I wanted to say, but I could tell he was daring me, setting a trap. I let him go on. We were maybe three miles out of Hooverton and Carnoe was looking more at me than the highway.

"Another sighter saw nine of them flying in an inverted pyramid formation, one-three-five, each one shaped like a convertible automobile and radiating an energy force. Craft movements, the person said, were either horizontal or vertical, precisely and perfectly so. And the pyramid of UFOs traveled as a unit. A lot of people just saw the beams of light, the sensor beams, and couldn't make out where they were coming from. It was not like light as we know it — neither wind nor dust particles passed through the beams. It was light transported four hundred and thirty-two million light years. I saw the beams, and I followed them through town in the truck. Once or twice they zeroed in on me. The crafts themselves were not tobacco can-shaped or automobile-shaped, they were exact rhomboids and only a few feet deep. There was a swarm of them, I couldn't tell how many, lights everywhere, lights carving up the ground. These people — these *beings* — were responsible for the missing cow hearts and sexual organs. They were Friggamites from Triamat in the Marduk galaxy. They had the bodies of wispy garden eels and their spaceships were filled with sand and water; Triamat is a global underwater desert. At home, they attach themselves to the ocean-desert floor and think. They do everything by thought waves. These wispy garden eel Triamatian Friggamites built their exact rhomboid spaceships by thought waves. This information was relayed to me in one of the light beams they shone on my truck — this very vehicle in which we sit.'' His voice remained unchanged, but his eyes were weeping freely. His face was red and wet. ''It was beautiful,'' he said. ''Otherworldly.''

We were inside Hooverton town limits. Townspeople waved at Carnoe, at Carnoe's rendering truck, from the sidewalks, from parked cars and moving ones. Kids waved from bicycles, a mail carrier waved a magazine. Carnoe nodded to them all, not bothering to dry his eyes.

''These are my people,'' he said. ''The Friggamites offered me the opportunity to return with them to Triamat, but I could not leave these people, my people.''

We pulled up in front of a long green steel building on the far edge of town, CARNOE RENDERING COMPANY. Boog's Mercury was parked off to the side of the building. I got out of the truck in a hurry, but then wasn't sure where to go. I kicked some gravel at the building, listened to it clack against the steel. Carnoe had slid across the seat and was leaning out the passenger side window. I started when he spoke, his head hanging down level with mine, his white sideburns suddenly brushing my cheek.

''The Friggamites wanted their own livestock. You see, they can think a cow, but these essential parts, the heart and reproductive organs, are unfamiliar to them. Therefore they must familiarize themselves with these vital parts so that they can just think them up in the future. Also, they must devise a way to keep these cows alive underwater. You've heard of manatees, of course — sea cows?''

''Sure,'' I said, taking a step away from him.

His tears had dried up except for a cluster of drops on his chin.

''Good,'' said Carnoe. ''They have asked me to recommend someone to return with them, someone who can assist them with their experimentation. I like you,'' he said, and retreated through the window.

Boog appeared through the sliding front doors of the building, drinking something in a yellow can.

''What took you two so long?'' Boog asked.

''We had some important business,'' said Carnoe. ''I didn't take the usual bypass road. Important business.''

Boog gave me the once-over, handed me the yellow can. Carnoe looked to the sky and said, ''I think I've found the right man for an important mission, Boog, a prime candidate.

Boog grabbed Carnoe by the shoulders and bent close.

''Have you cleared this with the Friggamites?'' he asked.

Maybe I looked to the sky too. They started laughing. Roaring and bellowing, refilling their lungs and letting loose again. I left them standing there, falling over themselves. I set out to do something adult, get back to the business at hand, make them feel silly. I unhooked the back door on the truck and gave it a hard push up with both arms.

Standing there live and breathing, front legs splayed, was Rooter.

If you can believe that.

MARNECK GOES HOME

SATISFACTION COLORING HIS FACE, Marneck says almightily, "Be seated and know."

He sits in the back of the new Dodge van with his younger sister Kate, both of them swathed in its blue shag carpeting and silver vinyl. They are making competitive jokes about educational furniture, a product advertised on the side of a big yellow truck they have just passed.

"Buy the Berlitz bed and sleep our language," says Kate, her eyes trolling his face for the right response.

He had forgotten her tense smile, how she reveals a half inch of bright pink gum above her teeth, and how she only has the one dimple, on her left cheek beneath her mole.

The van hurries east from Denver on Interstate 70, the foothills becoming lower, longer, thinning into the plains. Marneck watches the horizon stretch out and darken; the width and curvature of the windshield make it appear to wrap around them. There is a steadily approaching line of mottled bruise-colored clouds, routinely shattered by fork lightning. The storm is still well ahead, but thunder travels to the Rockies and echoes from behind.

"I remember now," he says.

But Kate cuts him short. "You can't remember now," she

says. "Bob's always saying that too. Now's now. If you can remember it, then it's then." She looks pleased with herself. "There, you thought I was all looks and no books, didn't you?"

Marneck's new brother-in-law, Bob, drives with his head stiff and businesslike. He talks to Mother Marneck about the size of her cukes, but he looks as though he's talking to the road. "I've been measuring ours by the length of my forearm, they're that big," he says into the windshield.

Sitting practically sideways in the passenger seat, Mother Marneck speaks only to Bob. She'd have to yell to be heard properly in the back above the air conditioning and tape deck, the latter playing music by a Swedish group who sing in English. She leans over and tells Bob she likes his music. "I don't mind that brand of noise one bit," she says. "Not like some of t'other."

Bob turns the Swedes up a notch and glances at his young wife in the rearview mirror.

Kate says, "Our doors make you stop and think."

"Doors aren't furniture," says Marneck. "It's educational *furniture*."

"Darnell Rence has a nice diningroom table he made from an antique barn door."

"Then," he says, "it's a table and not a door."

"That's being picayunish," she says in an exaggerated pout, "but I concede this once. Anyway, I give up. My head's pounding to beat sixty." She squeezes his hand and points out the side window at the storm. "We've been needing this, so long as we don't get too much."

He hasn't seen her in five years. She has finished school and married a man two years older than her brother. Marneck tries to picture his sister as Bob's wife. He sees Bob standing in loose underwear, shaving with a disposable razor while Kate sits on the toilet lid pulling on nylons.

"Mom's healing a couple of her houseplants with acupuncture," she says, poking Marneck's knee with her fingernail. "She has a book on it. The needles have to be pricked into certain parts of the roots. I swear it's done the world for her Persian violet."

When he moved away — as he boarded the plane for Vancouver — Kate handed him a box of notepaper and small square envelopes, both with cheering dachshunds along the borders. "You keep in touch," she said. He actually wrote her once using the notepaper, but was too embarrassed to use the envelope, to write his return address between a pair of cartoon weinie dogs in pep club sweaters. He placed the letter in a leftover Christmas card envelope, realizing after sealing it and walking ten blocks to the post office that the dogs were still visible through the cheap paper. He can't remember now whether he mailed it.

"First they tell you to play them classical music, then they tell you to talk to them, now some guy's telling everyone to prick them with needles," says Kate.

Mother Marneck hunches forward to push in the cigarette lighter. She is wearing a wig. Pieces of her own hair have fallen out from beneath it. They are the same color, but her real hair has less lustre.

Kate says, "The old brick two-story we just bought used to be a rooming house in the forties. It still has the brass numbers above the bedroom doors. We're thinking of leaving them up for something to talk about. What do you think?"

Bob steers the van into the Highwayfarer on the outskirts of Limon, saying he needs coffee. Mother Marneck orders cinnamon rolls for everyone without asking. They must be heated in a microwave because they arrive hot not a couple of minutes later. The waitress looks proud of them. They are huge, the size of hats, and Marneck's thick glasses steam over when he bends to look at his. "Creamy pecan," says the waitress, indicating the frosting. Her hostess tag has STARLET printed on it. Marneck wonders if that's really her name. If it isn't, why would she put that on her tag? STARLET. When he walked off the plane into the airport terminal this evening, he heard Bob say to Kate, "Here comes the celebrity."

He doesn't know what to say to Bob. Do you treat a brother-in-law like a brother? No, but there must be a set of rules. This new relative seems pleasant but temporary, like a sales-clerk or the waitress.

"I understand you sell tires," says Marneck.

"No," Bob replies, dunking the loose end of his cinnamon roll into his coffee, then trying to get his mouth around it without dripping on himself.

Kate laughs. "I told you that jacket made you look like a salesman. It's all that contrast stitching. The material too. He had these OPEC specials before we met."

"Sell, hell," says Bob, one side of his mouth full. "Maybe tenderized T-bone to hungry dogs."

"Bob does the big rigs," says Mother Marneck.

"I do repairs and new rubber installation. Probably put on a lot of the rubber out front of this place."

"Well," says Marneck, but he doesn't know how to continue. He thought a sentence would come out if he started it.

Sitting across from him, beside Bob, Kate suddenly looks sad and nervous. This isn't going like she planned.

"We're thinking of moving someplace different soon," she says.

Bob unravels more of his roll and examines the moist cinnamon and sugar inside. "Sure," he says. "That's why we bought a new house."

"Well," says Kate defensively, "we could hardly stay in the old one. The porch was coming detached and the floor joists were starting to crack."

"That's a fact," agrees Bob.

"Where are you thinking of moving to?" asks Marneck, hoping the question will settle her.

"First I've heard of it," their mother says.

''It is not,'' says Kate. Then she looks at Marneck and laughs. ''Afraid we'll move up closer to you and be a bunch of pests?''

Bob pulls the lid off the Thermos coffee pot and watches the steam for a few seconds before pouring himself another cup. Mother Marneck exhales, and the steam and her smoke rise together.

''It's too bad you couldn't get down for the wedding,'' Mother says.

''We had great rice,'' says Kate, fluttering her long fingers through the air until they land tapping on her head.

Marneck's mother is sitting on his right and holding his wrist tightly in her lap; he has to eat and drink left-handedly. The skin around his mother's eyes is red like she has been crying, but she hasn't.

''My matron of honor dyed it all different colors with food coloring,'' says Kate. ''It showed up in some of the photos, all this bright-colored stuff flying through the air at us. Mandy Peters was my matron of H — she used to be Mandy Buckingham, but she married Hot Donny Peters a year or two back. Donny's running his dad's motel. His dad had a heart bypass. You remember Mandy anyway! You used to drive out when she worked at A & W and talk to her between cars. I don't know what you had in mind — she was only a year older than *me*.''

''Her hair clashed something terrible with that orange uniform,'' says Mother.

Kate continues, ''She and Hot Donny actually live in one of the motel rooms. His dad kept the main suite.''

''Free satellite TV and swimming pool,'' says Bob.

''I suppose,'' says Kate. To Marneck: ''Can you fathom living your married life in a motel room?''

Marneck excuses himself and heads for the men's room. He stands and walks a couple of steps before his mother releases his wrist. As he weaves through tables he hears Kate say to their mother, "He's here for an entire week, Mom. I think Bob and I should take him to the lake for the long weekend."

When he returns his place has been cleared away and Bob is pulling money from a large wallet attached by a chain to his belt. Marneck's mother puts fifty cents under her ashtray. At the counter Marneck offers Bob a five-dollar bill but is waved aside.

"Bob always likes to pay," says Kate, linking arms with her mother and brother on the way to the van. "Don't ask me why."

It's raining lightly, but the worst of the storm has passed to the north. Marneck notes the silver surfer painted on the side of the van. He hadn't seen it when he got in at the airport. It's over a thousand miles to the nearest ocean, and they'll soon be driving further inland. The van belongs to Bob's boss.

After checking the air pressure in the front tires, Bob climbs in. Mother Marneck immediately pushes the tape back in and begins brushing her leg with an open palm in time with the music, occasionally anticipating a change and speeding up or slowing down, but the music remains steady. "Take a chance on me," she sings quietly with the Swedes.

Thirty or so miles down the highway, Bob says loudly, "Hon, I think maybe Fritz got hold of some bad meat."

"What's up with Fritz?" asks Marneck. Fritz is Kate's dachshund.

"He's just not acting himself," she says. "Bob wants him to die because he's jealous. I let him sleep between us. Bob built him a doghouse, but Fritz won't go near it. We threw his toys in there, but he won't even go in to drag them out again."

"I'll take him in to Dr. Nodden on Wednesday," yells Bob.

"Dr. Nodden is a taxidermist's best friend," Kate yells back. "No matter what you bring him, his advice is to put it down."

Bob shrugs.

''Screw his hide to the wall,'' says Kate.

Marneck assumes she's cursing either Nodden or Bob.

When they arrive in Colby the IGA supermarket parking lot is empty except for a police cruiser with three men sitting in it, talking. The other businesses in the shopping plaza are closed, but IGA stays open twenty-four hours. Bob guides the van into a space in front of the main doors while waving out the window and above the van to the police. They all wave back, then lean to see who's driving. Two of them say ''Bob'' slightly out of sync and the cluster of b's makes the third one laugh.

Once they are down out of the van, Mother Marneck hugs her son. He returns the hug, gently, afraid of hurting her, but also afraid of not squeezing sincerely enough.

''It's good to have you home,'' she says.

''It's good to be here,'' he says, feeling her wig move as she presses her head against his.

This is not the town where Marneck grew up. His parents moved here after he left home. There is nothing familiar in these surroundings. The empty parking lot extends beyond the lights, toward the town, foreign terrain.

''Go in first and surprise Dad,'' says Kate.

Bob has already started through the doors, but he hears his wife and steps back outside. Whistling ''Holly Holy,'' he props himself against the front of the van and scrapes insects off the headlights with the edge of a key.

The other three wait outside while Marneck goes in.

''I hope he eats the same things,'' Mother Marneck says to Kate. ''I already cooked some of his favorites and froze them so I wouldn't have to spend a lot of time in the kitchen.''

The store lights are so bright they seem to pulsate, reflecting off the white linoleum floor. There is a low hum from somewhere under the recorded music. Marneck walks past two aisles and glances down them, seeing no one, sensing no one in the store at all, and he considers what he would take from a grocery if he discovered one abandoned. Then a tall woman in an IGA smock and blue jeans steps out from behind a cash register.

"Help you find something?"

"Hal Marneck?" Marneck says.

"I'll page."

"No. Don't. I'll look around. It's kind of a surprise."

"Try down aisle eight," she says, tossing her head to the left. "If he's not there, try back in Dairy. We got a load of cheese about shift change."

"Thanks."

"You bet."

As he heads for aisle eight Marneck hears the electric doors open and footsteps, hushed voices, and he knows they have decided it is safe to come in. He doesn't turn to tell them otherwise.

His father is there, straightening and dusting cereal boxes. He's whistling, but not to the music from the overhead speakers. Quickly Marneck is beside him, slightly behind, reaching for the box his father is dusting.

"I'll take these if they're clean," he says.

Holding his feather-duster above the next box, his father turns his head, sees his son, smiles, dusts his son's shoulders. The feathers feel like moths' wings against Marneck's neck. He thinks about embracing his father but sees the boxcutter and price-stamping device hanging from the man's belt. There is loose skin along his jawline and a small scar near his right eye. Five years.

"How you doing?" his father asks, shaking his hand vigorously.

"Fine. How about yourself?"

"Oh, fine."

"What're you doing working graveyard?"

"They said I was the only guy they could trust."

Mother Marneck has her son by the wrist again.

When they get home, Marneck has to ask where his room is.

"We moved everything from your bedroom at the old house into a room upstairs at the end of the hall," his mother says. "Ignore the wallpaper and it's almost the same. About the same size."

Fritz races out of the kitchen, barking madly, wearing a tight green sweater over his long body. The dog leaps up at Kate, twisting himself in the air.

"Hot weather for sweaters," says Marneck.

"I know that, but he was shivering like crazy before we left this morning," she explains. "Go see big brother," she tells Fritz, "go see big brother."

Bob snatches Fritz up and tosses him out the front door. "Better go see a man about a tree," he says.

The bedroom is carpeted in thin rust-colored pile, with alternating American flags, bald eagles and crossed muskets on the wallpaper.

"'O say can you see...,' huh?" his mother says, opening a window.

"I'll say," says Marneck.

"If it's too much, there's a couch in the basement I can make up."

"No, no, this is great." He looks out the window, but it's too dark to see anything. The air is filled with the rattle of locust trees. He remembers throwing the seed pods like boomerangs as a boy, half expecting the next one he threw to return, believing it was possible. Passing underneath the window, Fritz sees Marneck and yaps.

"We'll make your father take us out for breakfast when he gets off in the morning. He can sleep in the afternoon and you and I can talk. You've got to tell me everything." She opens his suitcase on the single bed and says, "There are hangers in the closet. No sense ironing what we don't have to."

"Hey," says Kate, stepping into the room. "You two up here saying the Pledge of Allegiance? They must have bought this paper at a Fourth of July sale.''

''Your brother says he'll make do. We'll have it changed by his next visit.''

''Take me for a walk,'' says Kate.

''You two can stay up forever if you're fool enough,'' says Mother Marneck. ''I'm going to bed.''

When they've said goodnight and their mother is out of the room, Kate says quietly, ''Did you notice? She's got contacts. Our mother getting contacts! That's why her eyes are so red. I think she puts them in wrong.''

As they walk down the hallway she whips her blouse back and forth from her chest, letting air down her neck. ''What did I tell you?'' she asks, pointing to a plant on a hall stand, the eye-ends of several needles poking up out of the soil. ''It's doing them so much good, I'm thinking of getting myself stabbed.''

''Where's Bob?'' asks Marneck.

''I sent him home. I told him I wanted to stay and talk to you all night. I've decided to keep Fritz at Mom and Dad's.''

She tells him she's an adulteress as they walk past the El Dorado Motel. Mother knows but Father doesn't. The man is a legal aide, divorced, no kids. Jerome. Jerome wants her to get a divorce and move in with him. She doesn't think Bob has any idea. If they could just move somewhere else, she thinks maybe they could work things out. They are just going two different directions right now. She hates Bob's work friends and they seem to sense it. They always ask for Bob straight away when she answers the phone, no banter. When she asks Bob what they phoned about, he just shrugs and says Nothing. She met Jerome at a community theater production, a Neil Simon thing about aging men. Bob wouldn't take her. Jerome had the seat next to hers and they talked during intermission. What does her brother think of his little sister now?

''You're taller than I remember,'' he says.

She puts her arm around him and steers him down a side street a few blocks until they reach a double-wide mobile home.

"Jerome's ," she says. "I'll be over early tomorrow, okay?"

Marneck watches her go inside and listens to the trailer door close with the vacuum sound like the doors on *Star Trek*.

He finds his parents' house but has to check the number on the mailbox to be certain. Fritz hurries through the door ahead of him. The dog has dead leaves sticking out of his sweater.

In the downstairs bathroom Marneck finds a half-dozen catfish swimming around in the tub. It's a trick of his father's. Once a month during the summer, when Marneck was growing up, his father would take the family to Trenton Lake. The catfish he caught he released in a holding pool — a chicken-wire pen set up near shore, the light galvanized wire carefully staked down. Marneck liked to walk around in the holding pool, letting the slick fish bump his legs, until his father would catch him and order him out. When it was time to go home, his father loaded his fish into large plastic buckets of lake water, one or two to a bucket. The catfish were kept in the bathtub until ready to be eaten. The family sometimes washed at the sink for two or three weeks. But Marneck didn't mind that. He spent hours beside the tub, watching the catfishes' broad, bobbing mouths form imagined words.

Marneck removes his clothes and turns on the shower to a soft warm spray. Standing among the catfish, their scaleless skin gliding against his legs, he reaches over the sink and turns off the light. Dark moving water and familiar whiskered fish — *here*, he is glad to be *here*, in the first sense of home.

D'OYLY AND BELLE ANN

BELLE ANN TOLD D'OYLY she'd give him a call after they'd both had some time to think things through.

"Listen, D'Oyly," she said, finished weeping, stood before him refreshed and determined, "I know I've become my own echo on this, but I want you to know how I full well realize the immeasurable weight of our problem and that I am the trouble-some root. I will definitely get it sorted out this time. I swear. Somehow I will. It's not you though, don't you ever think that."

He did think, quite often, *that*.

"It's as much me as it is you, Belle Ann. I obviously don't spark you, and it shreds my mortal heart."

D'Oyly threw his scarred suitcase into the back of the pickup and climbed gloomily into its cab. Screeching and pining filled his foreseeable future. He blew his wife a kiss from the callous hoof at the base of his fingers, and she, standing on their front step in pajamas and ski jacket, pretended to catch it.

He started to yell something chipper and optimistic out the driver's window, but the words fell to pieces in his chest. "*Ungth*," he blurted, his foot on the gas pedal, the thin skin of his ears feeling the approach of winter. He rolled up the window and drove himself away.

D'Oyly spent every nonworking hour for the next fortnight

holed-up in a one-room detached hut belonging to the Hacienda Hideaway Guest Home, a string of dissimilar constructions vaguely linked by adobe-look salmon-colored stucco exterior walls and tile-look corrugated roofing. A sharp chill came off the South Fork Speed River and rode steady drafts through the gaps around the doors and windows. Belle Ann Belle Ann Belle Ann; with my sinewy jungleman frame, my high skin surface-to-body weight ratio, I am not prepared for a return to the Ice Age. Belle Ann?

D'Oyly, tucked fully clothed, shoes and all, under the blankets on the hard single bed, thought of his wife, saw her wrapped in endless layers of wool-things, curled up on the deep-cushioned bench he himself had built for her in their bay window, a heater vent directly beneath her, a cat on either knee, a mug, most likely, of International Blends instant coffee steaming from her girlish fist. Her. Looking out. Sighful. Thinking of him? them? *it*? The curtainless window above his head shook.

Why this again?

Usual reason. The everpresent reason.

He could not now bring to mind one solitary additional flaw in their marriage. He tried. They enjoyed the same interests, the same TV shows, pottery, unglazed ceramics, all stained glass, a dislike of Mexican food, and mutual enthusiasm for early morning walks and novice bird-watching. They had complementary biorhythms. Press their bodies together at any angle and they fit — for each jut a perfect nook. He found that amazing and mysterious. Walking together, they took such different strides but kept the same pace. They were thick as thieves while ever he could curb his urges. His urges for his own wife!

How, he asked himself constantly, could she go through life like she had the basics covered? He explained to her time and again about his psychobiochemical needs, his naturally low frustration point, and how she was so beautiful in whatever mood whatever time of day that he could just.... And she reminded him of his impatience, insecurity and expanding pessimism. He devoted weeks to making loud noises and unfair comments, to flying off the handle. Then, inevitably, he'd come to it. "Belle Ann," he'd hear himself shout, "I can't continue this way and you *know* that! I cannot go physically unsustained for these great long stretches. I am not a sex fiend, or a degenerate, or a glutton, but I *am* your husband, Belle Ann, your loving husband."

She knew that. But nothing roused.

It had been the cause of eleven separations in eight years.

They would agree they needed time away from each other to think, and D'Oyly would move into the Hacienda Hideaway Guest Home and live off of canned soup and corn chips and flagellating remorse. After a few weeks, Belle Ann would call.

"I've made some honest findings and some personal discoveries," she'd say, "and perhaps we could review them at your convenience."

"I too," he'd reply, "have information essential to the case."

They'd talk themselves well into the night; talk until they were sure they understood something new about themselves and their problem; talk themselves out. They drew liberally from family histories and adolescent trials, from gut feelings and common knowledge, lifting those precious moments of understanding out of the air — poking, paring, focusing, framing.

Each time, they wanted desperately to understand. They took turns understanding. The giddy epiphanic insights boiled in them like welcome fever, and they clutched and cried and forgave and signed on again.

They'd begun to live for the moments themselves, D'Oyly understood now. Less time lapsed between break-ups, and they were more quickly reunited, excited by the process, each new understanding seemingly more intense. But their sexual relationship had not improved. The condition remained stable:

tabled.

This time, on the twelfth point of departure, he had pressured her — something they understood would only make matters worse. But this time he could no longer imagine *how* it might make matters worse. Something's broken, he told himself, you fix it or get a new one. Understanding that the thing's broken will never in a million years contribute to its repair. Things had to change, had to get fixed, or he didn't know what.

What was it about the bonds of matrimony that had neutralized her romantic interest in him? Was it being tied to one man, Belle Ann?

No, she insisted.

Was it sameness somehow?

No.

Was it the implication of sexual obligation?

She didn't think so.

Had he become an uncaring, clumsy or uninteresting lover?

No.

Then, had she fallen out of love with him?

No... yes... of course she loved him.

Did she feel attraction to other men? Or to, say, women?

No, and no.

To what, if any, degree could it be linked to financial worries? Work-related stress? Vitamin deficiencies? Climate?

She didn't know, but she didn't think — well, eight years!

Did she want a divorce?

No, she didn't really think that was the answer for her.

Maybe it *was* him. Maybe she should have an affair.

D'Oyly.

Well, what did she expect him to think? to do? What?

Maybe *he* should just go have himself an affair!

Maybe he should, he said, hurt and frustrated.

Go to it, sport.

He might.

She would try to understand. She thought she could. It

was her —

Belle Ann —

fault.

"I," he said, "don't want to have an affair. I want *you*, Belle Ann. I want no other."

"I would that I could reciprocate your want, D'Oyly."

"I would that you could too."

"I will give you a call," she said, "when we've both had time to think things through."

In his third week of thinking D'Oyly went in to work on his day off.

"Guys," he said, adjusting the timing on a Toyota, "My picture's hung upside-down. I've got my dirt above my sky, and is it any wonder I see only the dark side?"

"You need to get out," advised Duane, the head mechanic, who had heard enough.

"I am supposed," said D'Oyly, "to be thinking. I am supposed to be coming to grips with the crux of the matter."

Duane waved his screwdriver at the calendar above the main tool bench, at the Parts Pet of the Month. "Come to grips with some of that," he said.

The new man, Rube, winked at D'Oyly.

"I'm bonded to that woman like H to O," he told them.

Rube rubbed solvent obscenely onto his hands, wrists, and forearms.

"She may crease your trousers, son," said Duane, "but your fly needs soup."

He phoned thirty-four times that Saturday night, but there was no answer. He tried her mother's: No, and why didn't he just keep to himself a while, it was bluntly suggested. She might be at a neighbor's, he reasoned, or shopping or at a movie or might even, in her time of contemplation, have resorted to jogging again — in this cold? She will, he told himself, no doubt be home soon, I believe.

D'Oyly sat in his Hacienda hut shivering severely and staring at the black desk phone with its numbers scratched off. His thoughts spread and choked him like bindweed.

He had tried foreplay so unhurriedly as to be virtually unnoticed. He'd taken her for romantic drives, spun music for lovers, been dominant and submissive, demanding and begging. To what avail? Gifts, intimate apparel, flowers, perfumes, erotic films — a stumbling parade of failed attempts. Told power was the ultimate aphrodisiac, he sent letters to the editor of the local newspaper; railing, insisting, assaulting. He had humiliated himself, he recollected, in a thousand and one ways. He wasn't saying it was her fault. He'd never ever said "fault." She was who she was and the way she was just was, that's all. Some things just were. And, he concluded, if that's true, then who are these separations fooling?

Black wind. That was the view from his front window. Black on black. The black scattershot of life's debris blown through the night. A cold black blast of it forced from a crack and winnowed his hair.

I am a short punt, D'Oyly confessed. Kick me in the end zone.

He dropped to the floor and fired off thirty fingertip pushups. Huffing a bit.

I have lost substantial yardage, but I still have my legs. Twenty-nine, thirty.

He ran to the front desk and leaned over, looking wild-eyed at the clerk.

"Heat, if you please, caretaker! It is vital to my revival. I am about to stroll through the Promised Land and upon my return I expect to be saunified. Heat, waves of it. Gimme swelter!"

I am, D'Oyly decided, about to grow a spine.

He shined his shoes with hair gel, donned good jeans and a tight white turtleneck, introduced himself to the bathroom mirror and stepped back. "My phaser is set on stun. Beam me up, ladies."

At Jimmy's, in nearby Mahoxie, around two a.m., he woke up nibbling the left lobe of a savings and loan teller named Joan — Joan Minot Blitton — packed into Gloria Vanderbilts and perilously high, gloss-black heels, a red lipstick print on either shoe. He bobbed at her feet for a few minutes, wanting to steal a kiss.

When he sat upright again, the house lights came on. Couples shielded their eyes and made for the exits.

"I bank," said Joan Minot Blitton.

"I mechanic," replied D'Oyly, dipping a finger repeatedly in his beer.

She said, "I'm open-minded, kind-hearted, and not looking to be tied down with anything or anybody. I live for today and search for tomorrow."

"I," he said, "I believe in a free range, no-fault insurance, in detente and Dutch treat, in the new morality and the court of appeal."

She went missing for a second as she stood, entering the lights.

"I refuse to play games with people who keep score," she said. "Do you keep score?"

"No chalk."

They went to her place: a four-room suite filled with gym equipment and tumbling mats.

"I'm fit crazy," she said, stripping down to a zebra-striped leotard. *And the heels.*

His senses rushing to him, his body in cardiovascular Grand Prix, D'Oyly took in her tall entirety for the first time as she stilt-walked his way. "Heal me," he muttered.

She chewed off his buttons and braided his body hair. They played Dogs & Cats, Hammer & Claw, Dive & Surface, and did something on her rowing machine that made him see Norsemen.

The following morning, he woke alone in the unsterile gauzy light, comforter hanging off the foot of her bed and every window in the place wide open, single sheet starch-frozen. She'd left him a note on the back of a gas company bill. *It was sure good,* she'd written, *But don't tie me down, Okay? Nobody scored, remember? Ciao Ciao Ciao, Joan Minot Blitton.* He dressed quickly, experiencing deep scorelessness.

Returning to the Hacienda, he discovered another note, this one in a peach-colored ragpaper envelope doused in familiar Wind Song. Had the egress begun? Maybe, Belle Ann. Whatever you're saying here, maybe, but I need something concrete this time. I — oh hell. He opened the envelope with his thumbnail.

Dear D'Oyly, There is hope. Hope for me. I am speaking to Analysts, Palmists and Licenced Practical Nurses, as well as Religious Leaders and Laypersons. The essence of Physical Love is elusive and may never be mine, but our Painful Chasm has made it my Quest.
Love, B. A.

Chasm. Quest. You look here, Belle Ann. You look long and hard, and if you have something having direct and substantial impact on our grievous state of affairs, you shout. But no more wolf. Cry me no more wolf. Last night I performed in a manly way, in true testosterone glory. You should have witnessed my grandeur. Where the hell were you when I was dialing thirty-four times? I feel had, Belle Ann, in more ways than my remaining brain can fathom. I just feel taken. Am I making any sense? I'm asking myself if I'm making any sense.

If anything the room was colder than when he left the night before. There was no one to complain to at the front office. The door was locked. Surveying the motel parking lot, he saw his was the only vehicle there. My dear dear trying wife, do you know what it is like to be alone on a mid-December

Sunday afternoon in a cheap and vacant motel with a partially Spanish name? D'Oyly tossed himself to sleep: "Who am I to. She doesn't. Better days. Free advice." Troubled snoring.

His second extramarital encounter was with a four-feet-nine landscape architect from Rondoville. She was at once laid-back and vigorous, plain and butte, evaporation and precipitation. And, she informed him post-coitally, she was screening potential stepfathers for her shy sister Ellen's four kids, and Ellen a husband of course.

"You're right up there above the norm, for sure, Doyle," she said. "Would you mind dropping off a load of decorative rocks at a client's house for me, honey? I saw you had a pick-up. It's right on your way. That'd be great. I'll get back to you about Ellen."

D'Oyly did not drop off the rocks. He did not look back. He hauled the rocks to the Hacienda Hideaway Guest Home, where he sold them for five bucks to Mrs. Kidd, the owner, who, if she was to be believed, had just returned from Disneyland with her fat nephew Teton.

"The black on Mickey's costume was all sun-bleached," she said. "Didn't look at all real."

He discussed the likelihood of his ever knowing a warm night under one of her roofs, while he arranged hunks of mica and iron pyrite on the scrubby courtyard grass. His particular furnace, she claimed, was churning out about all the heat it was capable of churning out, and perhaps he was being a bit fussy for all he was paying — why didn't he put that big flat one over there. He did as he was told, and the two of them, snow flurries gusting around their heads, admired what lay new and dully shining upon the lawn. A decorative rock burro.

"That," said a genuinely moved Mrs. Kidd, "is an attraction. I'll send Teton over with more blankets. That furnace in your unit is an antique, worth a lot of money. I'd be grateful if you wouldn't do anything to bust it." She went inside.

Christmas passed. January — January averaged 24° and 1.1 inches of snowfall, the highest wind clocked 86 m.p.h. Teton emptied the other huts of blankets and gave them to D'Oyly.

"Not knocking my auntie," said Teton, "but I'd seek shelter elsewhere, I was you."

"I'm expecting an important call," said D'Oyly. "You see the switchboard's manned."

There was a record cold spell in February and the town was mentioned on the national news. With all those blankets, there was hardly room to budge.

"Not fit for a brass witch out there," Duane said one night at closing time. "You want to stay a night or two at the house with Darla and me, that'd be all right."

D'Oyly refused. Diffused and defused.

Over the next few months he made a project of meeting concerned, receptive women with whom he could spend his nights. It was, more than not, draining. He rarely made the suggestion successfully before midnight, and then there were expectations and stipulations. When he dragged into the garage one viciously mocking sunny Wednesday in April and heard Rube say, "Your wife called," he felt indefinite relief, plus submontane confusion.

"But she's derailed," Duane said apologetically.

"What did she say?"

"Things to boggle the minds of ordinary men."

"For instance?" D'Oyly requested.

"She talked about the burrowing behavior of nocturnal mammals —"

"The unbearable tension of harp strings," said Rube.

"Chiasmatic chicanery —"

"Shimmering waters —"

"Metal fatigue —"

"Praying mantras —"

"The whole truth —"

"Nothing but the truth —"

"Newly apparent paralogisms —"

"Shintoism —"

"Veda —"

"Buddha —"

"Allah —"

"Taking all of us to the mountain —"

"Which one of you," interjected D'Oyly, "took the call?"

"I did," said Rube. "'Cept he snatched it off me."

"Your glaring lack of telephone etiquette is why," said Duane.

"Is she home?" D'Oyly asked.

"Afraid not," said Duane.

Unclear precisely why, D'Oyly kneed the door of a Chevy Biscayne, creating a shallow crater.

"Looks like you've got something to hammer out," Duane said. He thumped D'Oyly on the chest. "She'll be home tomorrow evening, you sorry fool. She wondered if you might care to drop by. I said I thought you might. Now pound out that Chev — that was dumb." He grinned and pinched D'Oyly's southerly face.

"She say where she's been?"

He raked the grass in the body of Mrs. Kidd's decorative rock burro, polished its mica eye with his jacket sleeve.

"What's with you?" asked Mrs. Kidd. "You drunk?"

He stood before her singing "Homeward Bound," never having known most of the words, improvising enthusiastically.

"I must tell you," he said, "that come tomorrow I hope to believe I will no longer be lodged beneath your roof, madam. In fact, you feel free to rent it to some sorry other."

"Suit yourself. I've got vacancies out the ear until middle of June if things don't work out for you."

He found Joan Minot Blitton's home number in the directory, then struggled with the number-defaced dial on his room phone.

"I'm booked for the future, sweetness," he told her, "on the train transcendental."

"Oily who? Is that you, Marvin?"

Unable to sleep, he found himself watching a *Gilligan's Island* rerun in the lobby with Teton, nearly two a.m. It was the episode where the skipper gets bumped on the head and wakes up thinking he's Rudolph Valentino. Teton howled — that ungainly tub Skipper trying to seduce sultry movie star Ginger. D'Oyly couldn't see much humor in being an embarrassment both in regular life and in fantasy life too. He took a drive past their house, wishing he had a key, that him not being able to return until she called him wasn't part of their agreement, wishing he could be sitting there with everything perfect when she arrived. Back at the Hacienda, he spent some time rearranging the decorative rocks into what he imagined to be an expansive heart, but what in the morning appeared more like a pair of joined lungs, one slightly shriveled.

At morning coffee he slipped down to Sally's Floral for a half-dozen hothouse orchids, custom-arranged on a thick bed of dried grasses: splitbeard bluestem, witchgrass, switchgrass, foxtail millet and Japanese brome. "The grasses' beautifully tragic brittleness counterpunctuates the orchids' glorious natural warmth and softness, both touchwise and appearance-wise," Sally said. He carried them back to the garage, holding them well away from his body, not trusting the pressure of his own arms. "It's the lunar pull," Duane told Rube when D'Oyly asked him to store the flowers and grasses in his office safe for the rest of the day.

But soon he was idling by their house — his and Belle Ann's, painted a fine Pacific Blue — her car wasn't there. A neighbor waved. D'Oyly bobbed at the neck. He made another U-turn, and Ted Jerome's boy, Ellis, slapped a tennis ball against the door of his pickup. D'Oyly angrily rolled down his window to yell at the kid, but couldn't think what to say. Cool evening air jumped down his shirt, rustled through his greying chest hair and escaped out his rolled-up shirt sleeves. The lights went on.

The lights went on. In that house, mid-block, their strikingly blue house. Parked along the street, he saw Belle Ann's car, its heat still rising.

He peeked in the front window before knocking. Couldn't see much, couldn't see *her*. He knocked, rolled down his sleeves and buttoned himself at the wrists.

"D'Oyly," she said, guiding him inside like it wasn't his house too, leading him to a chair.

"I really thought we'd gone and done it this time, Belle Ann. I really did."

"It was a consideration, wasn't it?"

"Where'd you disappear to all this time?"

"I took me a thoughtful drive, D'Oyly. I wandered. The Painted Desert, White Sands, Truth or Consequences, Elephant Butte, Saguaro National Monument, Petrified Forest, Carlsbad Caverns, Four Corners. I spent time at centers of higher learning and about maybe a dozen municipal libraries. I took the tent-trailer, so I didn't spend much if that's what you're thinking. Never mind that."

"Belle Ann," he said.

"D'Oyly, I'm ready to swap talk. I have thought things through."

"Me too," he said.

She suddenly looked troubled. "Tell me, D'Oyly. I'll try to understand."

"Depart not from the path which Fate has assigned you." It was from a fortune cookie. He had broken many.

"I can't argue with that," she said.

"It's tough to," he agreed, then felt stupid and almost shy.

"The manifestations of love," Belle Ann began, "are almost legion, ranging from those of the infantile period up to those of sublimated maturity."

...?...

"I think we have experienced a good deal of those manifestations, don't you? I think there is no doubt we love each other. Can we, to start with, agree that love, essentially, is not the issue, D'Oyly?"

Something spun inside him. "I love you, Belle Ann."

"Well, I love you too," she replied, "but we have agreed that love is not the issue, correct?"

"Tell me," he wanted to know.

"Everyone, D'Oyly," she said, "everyone to a person has advised me that we cannot pretend to ignore, in our marriage, one of the primary manifestations of love — that being our problem. We can, it has been suggested to me by qualified advisors, break up or come together, attend to our needs outside the framework of this institution to which we have committed ourselves, or must strive honestly for the goal hitherto beyond our mutual grasp."

"Can't I come home, Belle baby?"

"You sure can. You can come home right this minute."

She led him toward an act of congress. She spoke to him of Freud, Maslow and Dr. Ruth, of up-to-date mood-related nutritional studies, the relatively slow evolution of the libido, local college outreach courses in erotic literature, and of the *Kamasutra*. "One night," she said, breathing moistly along his neck, stroking his thigh with her foot, "one night I will ask you to speak to me as a man should a woman of the Maharashtra." She embraced him powerfully, making a *sut sut* sound. "We will practice together Jataveshtitaka, the twining of the creeper; also, the climbing of a tree, the mixture of sesamum with rice, and the milk and water embrace."

Then the silence of busy tongues and occupied mouths.

This was what he wanted, wanted most, this. But its vibrancy, its waves, were easily quantifiable, shallow and — what he wanted most refused to go beneath skin-level, refused to sink in. They tried for over an hour, like anxious and deliberate first-time lovers, reeled themselves in and cast themselves out, exhaustion gradually prevailing.

"Hell," said Belle Ann.

"Hell and damn," said D'Oyly. "I don't know what's wrong."

"I do," she said. "We are stuck at the 'I Self' stage, when we should be at the 'We Self.'"

"'I Self,'" he said, lying on his side, staring into her hair.

"The most normal stage of human perception," she explained. "D'Oyly, we are caught between arousal and tranquility, between the ergotrophic and trophotrophic, as conscious-state research psychologists tell us."

"Caught between arousal and tranquility," he pondered.

"Don't you see? Dr. Hugo Zazen proposed the 'Self' scale in a book I'm reading called *From Me to We*. We could go either direction, D'Oyly. And it doesn't matter which way we go, we're getting away from the 'I Self.' To the right, there's tranquility, hypoarousal, and eventually enlightened integration with the world around us."

She was talking science, he comprehended that.

"And to the left of the scale, there's arousal, hyperarousal, and eventually the ecstatic states of mysticism and rapture...."

She was asking him to understand a lot, an awful lot, and a peculiar energy coursed through him, a raw, warming buzz, as he attempted to decode her message for his own understanding.

"We're caught right up the middle, right?" he asked.

"At the 'I Self.' Yes, as I understand it, that's our hurdle."

"And," he proceeded carefully, "if we can get *past* the 'I Self,' in one direction we experience arousal and rapture, and in the other, tranquility and enlightenment?"

"The 'We Self,' my loving husband. And I think we should try."

Wouldn't that beat all, he thought, flushed — I mean, if there's truth in it, if that's what it is: the 'I Self.' All this time and trouble. Well, my god. 'I Self.' Hardly a brick wall.

"D'Oyly."

About ten pounds light of nothing, an 'I Self.' All in our heads, she's saying. We can go right or we can go left, any damn way we please, we're busting free of the 'I Self.'

She was tired. One of her arms had already gone to sleep.

He was laughing to himself now, laughing at some wimpy little slip of thought matter called the 'I Self,' laughing at the simplicity of a thing once it's understood.

DEAF

ED PLACES HIS STOCKING FEET on the edge of Irv and Julie's coffee table and lets his muscles uncoil. He has long narrow feet with short toes. His wife, Mary, has long prehensile toes. She can pick up dropped pencils or collect the children's discarded clothing without stooping. Sometimes he sees her as a different species from himself, closet arboreal and full of secret longings.

"All snakes are deaf," he says.

"Who among hell's apes cares," says Mary, reaching for her bourbon and Seven.

It is missing from the coaster where she set it down. Looking around the room, she notices only young Karen is holding a drink.

Karen is the reason they're here. Julie and Irv wanted to have their new neighbor over for drinks and thought she might be more comfortable in a larger group, so they invited Mary and Ed to stop by.

Mary doesn't like this Karen's nose one bit, the way the point of it dips when she speaks. At least the girl hasn't said much.

"They're deaf," repeats Ed. "You can talk at them through a bullhorn and they won't hear word one. That whole idiot business of snake charmers coaxing up cobras out of baskets is a lot of bunk."

"No one's arguing with you, Ed," says Mary.

"Well, how's it done then if they can't hear the music?" Julie asks.

"I don't know," he says. "I'm not saying snakes aren't a mystery. I'm just telling you they're deaf."

Ed's knowledge of snakes derives from three years spent working for Doc Chekes at The Reptile Villa, south of Kendora. Chekes was old and short and walked stiffly around the grounds in heavy pants, legs reinforced by fine wire mesh. That was nearly fifteen years ago. Ed graduated high school and was trying to avoid going into refrigeration and air conditioning with his father. His last year at Reptile Villa, Ed contributed part of his wages to help pay for the white mice Doc ordered up from Toledo twice a month. The bypass was built and business fell off dramatically along the old highway. They released the more common snakes because Doc couldn't afford to feed them. They turned them loose in the field behind the Villa and pointed them away from the highway.

"It's a fact," Ed continues. "But when Doc first told me, I thought he was just giving me a poke. The next few days, I waited around until he'd gone home for the night and I was supposed to be locking up, then I'd walk over to the main pit and scream at them. I got down on my hands and knees and yelled into their hole until I was blue. You know, to see if they would react at all."

"Did they?"

"Blind nothing. Business as usual. I even brought my referee's whistle and tried that on them. Nothing at all. I couldn't believe all those guys were deaf as rocks."

"Maybe they can only hear on unusual frequencies," suggests Irv, carrying another tray of drinks into the room.

Ed shakes his head. "Deaf."

Mary takes her drink politely, stirs it with her finger, and sucks the sweetened alcohol from her skin.

"You're bordering on deafness yourself," she says. "Yesterday Mike comes home from school and tries to tell you what one of the boys told him about homos, and you don't even look up from the Sears catalogue. You just tell him you don't have the money for it."

They all laugh.

"Well, I don't," says Ed.

Mary realizes she's spoken to Ed several times since they arrived; she curses herself.

Julie turns to Mary and says, "Listen, do you have that catalogue? I can't think now which store. The one that has the photo of the guy modeling boxer briefs — only he's advertising a little extra out of one leg."

"Really?" Karen asks, smirking. "Bring it out. Let's see."

"I haven't seen it," says Mary.

"I don't have it myself," Julie says. "I just read about it somewhere. It seems neither the photographer nor the store noticed until it was too late. They'd already been printed up and half mailed out. Can you imagine?"

"I wonder if he knew he was peeking?" says Karen.

Julie smiles at her new young neighbor. The girl hasn't told them much about herself. She was born in Swift Current and one day the wind took most of the washing off her mother's clothesline and held it pinned high against the side of the house next door. Her father had to fetch a ladder to retrieve the laundry. They looked like paper doll clothes pressed there waiting to be cut out, she said.

Having a younger woman for a friend will be nice, thinks Julie. Mary talks about nothing but golf and television. Julie would like to talk about the G spot, music, the economy, fashion....

"I'll tell you something," says Ed.

"Don't bother," snaps Mary. She drinks from her bourbon and refuses his eyes.

"If it was Irv or I talking about the photos we'd seen in the women's scanties section, we'd be taking some flak here. Am I right?"

Julie says, "I'm sorry, Karen. You've hardly met us and here we are off on this kind of talk."

"Oh, I'm no prude," the girl says. "Go on and don't you worry."

"I'm really glad you could come over tonight."

"It was great of you to ask. I might have been anybody."

Karen wonders if Julie caught her staring at Ed. There is something about him that reminds her of her cousin Doyle's Mediterranean-style furniture — the darkness, for one thing. He's not a big man, but his body looks strong and his angles refined. And his dark tanned arms, covered in thousands of short black hairs — like the custom specks on the furniture's wooden arms and legs. Flyspecks, Doyle calls them.

"Did you meet the people who lived in the house before you?" Julie asks, noticing how thin Karen's eyebrows are. Not plucked narrow, but naturally sparse. She is petite and athletic-looking. She sits, thinks Julie, like a gymnast probably sits.

"They'd been moved out a week when I first looked at the place," Karen replies. "Have you seen the house? You should come over and have a look. The colors they painted the upstairs bedrooms, my god, I don't know how they slept."

Ed says, "They had a peacock over there for a while, didn't they, Irv?"

"That peacock didn't last long. I don't know what the earth became of it," says Julie. "But they had a small dog which used to throw itself against the side fence between our yards."

"I think it was trying to climb over," says Irv. "We'd be out barbecuing and we'd hear this wham against the fence and lots of scratching on the boards. It was a little distracting."

Julie holds up her empty glass for Irv to see, but he's rubbing his forehead.

"I'd guess," says Karen. "I had two canaries before I moved out here. But I decided to leave them with one of my aunts. I was worried they wouldn't stand the trip."

"Birds aren't the best travelers," says Julie.

"Ed might get you a deal on a snake," jokes Irv.

Ed swings his head sadly. "You wouldn't find much of a selection if you went out there now. The couple who bought the place off Doc seem to be more concerned with the cafe part."

"Nobody wants a neighbor who keeps snakes anyway," Mary declares bitterly.

"As long as they don't throw themselves at my fence, what do I care," says Julie. She stands and starts loading the tray with empty glasses. "I'll fetch us another round," she says.

Ed grins. "You just want to remember: if it runs away, it'll do you no good driving around the block hollering its name out the window."

When Julie flips the kitchen light on, Mary catches the flash in the corner of her eye and winces. It burns for a second, though she has no idea what happened. The alcohol has made her warm and hungry and has brought out certain things in her perception, blurring most others. She knows this stage of drinking and likes it.

There are zippers running all the way up the outsides of Karen's pants to her waist. Why would anyone make pants like that? she wonders. Listen to stupid Ed keep using the word "just." "I just don't know, Irv. I mean, just look at a fella like him. Just look." She watches Karen remove her wire-rims and set them down on top of a *Time* magazine, on the stand next to her chair. Looking through one lens, Mary sees the last two letters magnified, as if the magazine's title is *ME.* She has thumbed through the one called *Self* at Shoppers Drug Mart. They all...all those magazines want you to improve yourself, like nothing about you goes right if left to its own natural inclination. What did we do before we had magazines to guide us?

Rising up from her seat ever so carefully, and paying strict attention to her balance until she's standing, Mary considers whether to tell Julie — of course she'll tell Julie — what that selfish fool husband of hers has done. She smiles and nods to Karen as she passes, but the girl is talking to the men.

He is pure-D fantastic! *God! Listen!* Listen to this Ed, thinks Karen. Deaf snakes, this is just great. None of the men back home talk to her nor listen. They either want to jump it and scoot, or they suck up and whine like you're their mother.

"Ed had a vasectomy last week," Mary says as she enters the kitchen. "Can you believe that?"

Julie hands her a fresh drink.

"I've heard him tell you he was going to," she says.

Leaning against the kitchen table, Mary looks to Julie as though she is falling away. She wants to put a hand out and grab her.

"It's usually the woman who decides how many children, isn't it? I don't know. My mother did," says Mary. "Shouldn't be his lone decision."

"You must've talked about it."

"You can imagine talking to Ed. I mean, you can't. It's always a joke. You don't know what he's serious about and what he's just saying. He told me several times he was going to have it done, but I thought he was just trying to get a rise out of me, so I wasn't going to give him the benefit. You know how they play that game."

"Surely he said, 'Today's the day.'"

"I've never actually known a man have it done, have you? Most think it's like gelding — cut nuts or something. Christ! He walks in the door a little early, pats me on the ass, and says, 'I just pruned the family tree.' Jesus and Martha! It took me a minute to figure what the hell he was talking about. He'd obviously rehearsed that dumbass line all the way from the doctor's office. I don't know what he expected. I just felt sick."

"What did you say to him?"

"Nothing." Mary rubs her thumb across the vinyl back of a kitchen chair until it becomes too hot to continue. "I couldn't think of one thing to say. I kept thinking about all that *Our Bodies* crap. Our Bodies, therefore Their Bodies. We have two good kids, I said to myself, and he's been talking about this for months — I thought he was joking, but he wasn't...that's all."

Julie pushes some stray hair behind Mary's ear and tops up her glass with bourbon.

"I still want to run into him with the car," Mary says, "or slap at him like there's no tomorrow. But that's stupid. If I just didn't have to hear his voice rattling on like nothing happened."

"I don't know," admits Julie.

When they return to the living room, Karen is sitting with her legs tucked under her, playing with the zipper on one leg, absently hiding and revealing her pale calf.

"My aunt told me about this woman in some town in Montana," she is telling Ed and Irv. "The woman took her little boy to one of the discount stores to buy him a coat. Well, the salesclerk brought over this coat for the boy to try on. But every time the boy pushed his arm into the sleeve, he pulled it out again and said, 'Ouch, Mommy, it hurts!' Of course the mother just keeps telling the boy not to be silly and to try the coat on. The salesclerk's getting impatient too. After a few minutes of this, the clerk notices blood on the boy's wrist."

"I'm sorry we left you alone with these guys, Karen," says Julie, passing around glasses.

"Ssssh," says Ed.

After resuming her seat on the couch, Mary stares at Karen's mouth. How perfectly horizontal it is when she stops talking. Mary wishes the girl would shut up.

"There was a small snake in the sleeve of the coat," continues Karen. "The coat had been shipped all the way from Hong Kong with a snake up the sleeve. And it had bitten the poor boy five or six times."

"God!" exclaims Julie.

"Was it poisonous?"

"I don't think so."

"What kind was it?"

"A Hong Kong coat-sleeve snake," Mary says sarcastically.

"I don't think I ever heard," Karen replies.

She has unzipped her pant leg above the knee and is pulling at a loose thread. Mary watches her and imagines the entire zipper coming unstitched, the material opening to the waist, falling away like shed skin.

"We should head home soon," says Ed.

"Me too," says Karen.

"Where have they got you working this week, Ed?" Julie asks, hoping to draw out the night until Mary is drunk enough to sleep.

"THE OATMEAL TOWER," he booms grandly.

Ed works as a welder for a subcontractor.

"What an ugly building," Julie says. "It's so plain. Bland."

"Like oatmeal," says Irv.

"I just fuse the bones," says Ed. "No say over the cosmetics."

Karen says, "I didn't think anyone ate oatmeal anymore."

"If Home Hearth can afford to put up a new office tower, someone's eating it."

"What's that stupid slogan they use?"

"Feel your oats," Ed says, shaking his head.

"It's not as bad as the one Quaker's been using all these years," says Irv.

"What?"

"What?" asks Julie.

"Nothing is better for thee than me."

"What's wrong with that?" asks Ed.

"Remember that chubby Quaker on the packages...and now on the TV bit he still says, 'Nothing is better for thee than me.'"

"So?"

"Think about it. What he's really saying is: 'Eat me!'"

"Jesus, Irv," says Julie.

"It sounds like something Ed would have come up with," says Karen.

"I wish," he says.

Mary rolls her glass between her palms and finds herself staring again at Karen's two-thirds bare leg. The girl looks like she never sets foot outdoors, she thinks.

"My Uncle Deac," Karen begins loudly, then takes control of her voice, quietening it, pacing herself, "my uncle and aunt have this farm. I used to go out and spend summers when I was young. Uncle Deac kept bags of oats for the horses — Nugget and Mr. Dillon. Anyway, I was with him one afternoon when he reached in for a handful of oats. Well, he pulled out this snake!"

Ed asks, "What kind?"

"A bull snake, I think."

"Snake bull," mutters Mary.

"A-K-A gopher snake or pine snake." Ed blushes at his expertise, but he feels good, an authority.

"Uncle said it was harmless. It was big and black and had a bulge in it which he said was a mouse."

Yes, thinks Ed, it would have been. He recalls feeding white mice to Doc's snakes. He can visualize several of them digesting their lumps. Peaceful, undulating. He'd often wanted to reach down and pinch those lumps, flatten them out a bit. Watching the snakes' distorted forms made his throat feel thick.

"Genus *Pituophis*, that's one I remember," he says. "We had signs for the tourists."

"We'd better be getting home," says Mary.

Ed says, "It looks like we're already paying the sitter to spend the night." He turns to Irv. "Dollar an hour per kid to watch restricted movies on pay TV. And she gets an extra five if we're home past midnight and she has to stay over."

"Good thing we're only paying her for sitting two." Mary glares.

"Okay," he says, leaning back in his chair.

"Mary," Julie says calmly.

"Go ahead, Mary," says Ed. "Here we go. You've been wanting to say something. Well, go ahead. Here we go."

"I don't need to say anything to you."

"The hell you don't," he says. "The hell you don't."

Julie watches him tense up, even his voice constricts.

"You've been pacing around out of my reach since that very afternoon. Well, come on. You've got an audience."

Irv finds himself siding with Ed, though he has no idea what they're talking about. Mary just seems drunk and unreasonable. He looks directly into the lamplight, in the corner between Karen's chair and the end of the couch where Mary is sitting. He had meant to look at Mary, try to gauge her anger, but turned his head too far. There is only white for a couple of seconds, until his eyes adjust and widen his field of vision, then he sees both Mary and Karen. Karen is holding the knuckles of one hand against her chest. Mary's head and neck are trembling, almost bobbing.

"You might as well take a bite out of me here in public," Ed says. "Here in front of our friends."

"You just worry about your snakes," Mary says spitefully. "Tell us some more dingass snake stories, Ed. Talk to the girl, why don't you."

"Mary!" Julie says abruptly.

"She's safe. He's perfectly goddamn harmless. Like her idiot bull snake. He could crawl all over her and not do her no harm."

"All right, Mary," says Ed rigidly. "We're going home. Now."

"You've got a problem, lady," says Karen.

Mary swings her arm violently, sending the lamp flying

onto Karen's lap. She hears nothing after the hot explosion of the light bulb, but sees Ed leap from his chair and strike her. There is little pain, just a deep warmth where his hand lands. When he steps back, horrified, Mary sees Karen shove the lamp to the floor and take off across the room with her unzipped pant leg flapping like loose bandages.

A year from now, when Julie is over at Karen's doing aerobics to a workout record, Karen will give her a playful hip bump and say, "I want to have a child and I'm thinking of asking Ed to donate for it."

"Donate?" Julie will ask.

"You know, be the sperm donor. Mary wouldn't have to know."

"I swear," Julie will say. "There's none so deaf as those who won't hear." And she will explain Ed's limitations.

"Too bad," Karen will say. "I think the man's a charmer."

CLASSIC JURASSIC

IGNACIO WAS AN IMPULSE BUY. Martins, the biological supplies salesman, got him for me — a twenty-one-inch Banded Basilisk, a lizard whose natural haunt is anywhere from Mexico south to Ecuador — a real beauty. I'd been reading articles on facultative bipeds, and when Martins came to take the monthly order for our department at the university, I added, "and a Banded Basilisk," making it sound whimsical, *a Banded Basilisk and a partridge in a pear tree.* He checked his computer printout inventory list and quoted me a price. I thought I was asking for something rare and forbidden. (How many of these animals does his company move?) "Live or preserved?" he asked, pencil ready. And I said, "Live." And he said, "Better give me ten weeks on that," and shook my hand.

Ignacio stops his patrol and races at me from the back fence, almost forty yards away, his chin tilting upward like the nose of a plane. He's on his hind legs and pushing powerfully at the ground. *Rise up! Leap!* His lesser front legs wave at the air. He bounds twice, entirely airborne, and I find myself dipping at the knees and willing him *up!* I don't, of course, expect him to fly, but I do think longer, higher leaps are attainable. Coming toward me, his wide stance makes his legs appear to go around three hundred and sixty degrees with each quick stride.

Then he is clinging to my pant leg and taking mealworms from my fingers. The tip of his tongue feels like the rolling ballpoint of an ink pen — probing, moist, solid. I've only had him for five months, and he's been eating from my hand for two. "I don't know what you've done to the bugger," Horenson from Anthro said when he saw him. "In Colombia they disappear like smoke the moment they catch wind of a human." Horenson the brave. Horenson spent all of 1974 pacing the Magdalena River in hope of hearing one surviving syllable of Chibcha Indian, but he wouldn't go near Ignacio. He commented from inside the house. "I don't strictly approve of what you're doing here, MacDonlaigh," he said. "For one thing, you provide all the food for this creature and what's it supposed to do with itself?"

"Become more ambitious," I said.

Ignacio chews his mealworms slowly, keeping his eyes fixed on my mouth, the origin of threatening behavior. The wide, vivid band of yellow along his sides swells as he swallows. He is a dark olive color, with a bony ridge running the length of his back. I try for a nonthreatening lizard look: my eyes half closed, the corners of my mouth at mid-cheeks. And I'm caught at it by my daughter.

"Great impersonation," says Di. "Want me to put your hair up in a crest?"

I lift the heavy lizard from my trousers, amazed at how totally unconcerned he is with my hands. He continues to stare at my mouth.

"He really took off today," I say, maintaining the look.

"I tried to feed him a tomato hornworm this morning," she says, "but he spit it up."

On the ground again, Ignacio hunts a string of live mealworms I've spread near the porch.

"Did Lalla call?" I ask.

"She says she still hasn't found a place and that she thinks her landlord is a witch."

"Warlock." He's the owner's son, a landlord by birth. "She says he's been going through the tenants' trash, finding thing to burn. She says he stands by the incinerator half the night chanting into the flames."

"Too young," I say. "Must be an apprentice warlock."

"He's twenty, Dad."

"A warlock wouldn't drive a Trans-Am." I don't believe he's a warlock, and I don't believe she believes he's a warlock, but I like talking to my daughter.

"He has a Harley now too," she says.

"Great."

"And he rides it around the pool with a black cape on."

"Di," I say, letting her know I know she's touching up the story, which she often does if she thinks I'm not sufficiently impressed by what she's saying.

"No, *really*," she says impatiently. "Lalla says he's trying to pick up the Compessi twins. They're in her Historical Geology class. 'Buxo deluxo!'" She giggles at Lalla's description of the twins. "Anyway," she says, "he's always down at the pool on his motorcycle or burning things and he still hasn't done anything about her cable. All she gets is the picture from the airport channel and the sound from PBS."

"Is she coming over later?"

"She said she didn't know yet."

"Did you tell her our latest offer?"

"She pretended not to hear."

We both want Lalla to move in. It's serious, the three of us, and she's been wanting to get out of her apartment since spring, since her landlord moved to Florida and left his son in charge. Di proposed the idea to her a couple of months ago, without asking me first, though I'd been thinking a lot about it as well. Lalla is understandably hesitant: "...with an undivorced man, an eleven-year-old would-be sitcom actress, and a giant yellow-banded lizard? Let me think it over." She is currently looking for another place of her own.

"I hope the warlock keeps it up and she just can't find another place," says Di.

"There are plenty of places."

"Well," Di says tersely, "Lalla says it's not because of me, so it must be you, Dad."

She goes back into the house, feigning hurt. As she walks across the kitchen, I notice she bought the elf boots, Peter Pan Getaway Boots they're called in grade six.

"Maybe warlock's using voodoo to keep her in his building," I say. But I don't think she hears me. I know witchcraft and voodoo are different things and she probably does too.

Lalla predates me by thirty-five million years. She teaches Triassic: the supercontinent breaking up, first dinosaurs, maybe first mammals (we disagree), from two hundred thirty to one hundred ninety-five million years ago. I teach a second semester course on the Jurassic and the Cretaceous: warmer climate, climax and death of dinosaurs, appearance of the first bird, from one hundred ninety-five to sixty-five million years ago. I was drawn to the Jurassic by the first bird — by the *idea* of the first bird, of first flight. Lalla and I bicker sportingly on the origin of avian flight. She sees things swooping down from trees; I see them rising up from the ground.

Most paleontologists subscribe to the arboreal theory of flight, believing primitive ancestors of birds were tree-dwelling animals which developed the increasing need and skill to leap from branch to branch, and from tree to tree. This is the widely embraced theory. The ones which didn't fall and kill themselves survived and multiplied. I support the much less popular cursorial theory, that reptiles went from being quadrapedal to bipedal, running on two legs at high speeds — like Basilisks and Australian Frilled Lizards — and with elongation of forelimbs and enlargement of scales, they formed thrust surfaces, early wings, and lifted themselves higher and higher. Lalla's considered opinion has become her nickname for me. "Flap," she says.

When I get inside, pages from the telephone directory have become Magicians' Hats and Japanese Schoolgirls. Sixteen pages of the *TV Guide* are Trees On A Hillside. Di has colored the trees blue with a felt-tip pen, and the rigid hills bear tiny photographs of Tom Selleck, Joan Collins, and other TV people. She senses me about to say No when she reaches for more pages and says, "I'm gonna ace origami. I have to make up for batik. Did I bomb batik!"

She's all bony white elbows and fingers, pleating, swiveling, squash-folding and crimping, her head bowed.

She says, "Mrs. Pinatel says the mother is the art and the father is the craft."

Mrs. Pinatel! Who last week told the class: "Children are the fruit and parents are the trees, and the best fruit stays with its trees until fully ripe." Lalla insists the woman studied art at a bible college. She offered to have a talk with Pinatel when the teacher started asking questions about Di's mother.

"I bet you look just like your momma," Pinatel said.

"Maybe," said Di.

"Does she have that red-red hair?"

"I guess."

"You guess? You'd be color-blind not to notice, wouldn't you?"

"I remember it more as blonde."

"What color is it now, honey?"

"I don't know."

Pinatel sensed grave moral injustice. "Are you from a broken home, darling? Are your folks divorced?"

"Separated."

"Landsakes! Where ever is your momma, dear? Why on earth aren't you with your momma?"

"She's singing."

"Pardon me, dear?"

"Singing. She's a singer. She went away to sing."

Pinatel hugged her madly. "You dear forgotten lamb."

Pause. ''Does your momma dance too?''

It goes on. And I suspect it's ongoing. Di did twenty minutes for us the night after the first question period.

She asked Lalla not to cause a fuss. Her marks have gone up this term and she was allowed to skip haiku. ''I told Pinatel it all sounded like Mom's song lyrics.''

Di's mother, Marla, sang me through graduate school, but pregnant and living in Whitehorse, where I'd accepted my first teaching position, she soon became miserable. After Di was born, Marla would go into the nursery at night and sing a set from her act. When I'd call her away, she'd do her break song before leaving. We separated when Di was four. One morning she walked into the kitchen, where Di and I were drawing dinosaurs from a paleontology textbook, and asked tearfully, ''Are you two old enough to look after yourselves?'' ''Old as dinosaurs,'' replied Di. I circled my pterodactyl and slashed a line through it. It was not a surprise, and there was no disagreement over what Di would do. Marla is a singer, she needed to sing. We'd talked about it. I can live with that, I said. Di has a glossy promotional photo of her mother taped to her mirror. In it, Marla is singing her heart out to someone directly beneath the photograph. She appears sincerely happy.

Right now our daughter is picking the steak I've been seasoning up off the cutting board and peering underneath.

''Fish is better for you than beef,'' she says.

''See anything?'' I ask, dropping beans in the steamer.

''Gore,'' she says.

I wipe my hands on my apron and point to the screen door, where Ignacio is hanging. He sometimes climbs up to catch insects around the porch light. But I haven't turned the light on yet. I always expect the screen to pull loose from the weight. There is still some sun left, enough to throw his enlarged shadow into the dining room.

Di shouts, ''Ig!'' She marches over and begins thwacking his claws with her middle finger, until he leisurely backs down, his long tail testing the ground.

"I told Pinatel about him," she says, collecting her origami figures and finding perches for them around the room.

"What did she say?"

"She thought I meant a lizard like a skink."

"Rhonda's seen him, what did she say?"

"Rhonda's not in our class. I held out my hands to show Pinatel how big he was, but she just laughed. I should take a Polaroid."

"Good idea."

"What would be really great is to walk him into class on a leash." She tries to spin a mushroom like a top.

"Forget it," I say. We've had this talk before.

"I know. I know," she says. "Wouldn't be fair to Ig."

Lalla phones that night while I'm in the bath and Di talks to her for thirty minutes or more before tossing the receiver into the bathroom, leaving the rest of the phone outside the door. I have to roll over and slide almost out of the bath to reach it. I can hardly see through the steam. The dry air, from the couple of seconds the door was open, crosses the room and hits my back and neck, and it makes me think of the weather maps on the evening news, where the dry air cuts through the moist air and the moist air wraps around, which makes me think of that finger game: scissors cut paper, paper wraps stone, stone breaks scissors.

When I pick up the receiver, I say, "Paper."

"What about feathers?" asks Lalla.

I have drawings of feather development strewn through the house, and I wonder what Di has told her.

"Feathers," I say.

"The subject is feathers."

"Mayr, 1960: development of feathers for coloration. Parkes, 1966: development in conjunction with flight. Ostrom, 1974: feathers as insulation to retain body heat. Regal, 1975:

feathers as heat shields.''

''But you're working on something else.''

''The real untold story.''

''I can see hair,'' she says. ''A further development of cilia perhaps...'' Playful sardonicism. ''... but I always thought feathers were a strange piece of work. Why feathers, Flap?''

''Highly confidential.''

''Come on. Out with it.''

''It's just too big, Lalla.''

''How big is it?''

''A *really* big theory, right here on *R* stage....''

''That big!''

''Soon to shake up the entire paleontological community.'' I know too well how they'll react.

''So rattle me,'' she says.

''Big,'' I repeat.

''Bigger than hair?''

''Way bigger than hair.''

''Give a hint?''

''No hints.''

''Hint?''

''I haven't refined the idea yet.''

''Hint?''

''Tell me about Warlock.''

She's in her goading mode. ''Hint hint hint hint hint?''

''Lalla.''

''Hint hint hint hint hint hint hint hint hint.''

I confess. ''Insect nets,'' I tell her. ''Insect nets.''

She stops.

''Feathers developed as insect nets.''

Her reaction, once she's confirmed my seriousness, combines stifled laughter with professional advice. ''Ground control,'' she says.

When I begin to elaborate she sounds fatigued and says she really can't grasp anything substantial tonight. I ask if she's okay.

"Sure," she says. "I'm a hostage in my own home, but I'm okay."

"Let me talk to this guy," I say. "I'll talk to him." She has previously forbidden me to intervene. It's territoriality, she claims. And she's not territory.

"I spent two full hours talking to Boy Landlord," she says, her voice stressed. "Yesterday he informed me he didn't have to provide my cable TV because it wasn't written in the lease. He said it was between me and the cable company. So I called cable. They said they couldn't do any repairs without his approval — something to do with it being his property and the original contract being in his father's name. I told them just to shut mine off then, and they said *he'd* have to make that decision, not me. Can you believe that? I unhooked everything myself and stuffed the cable connections and the converter in the kid's mailbox."

"You haven't found another place?"

"I'm looking. I'm looking. I told him I was looking too and that I'd be moving out soon, that I was giving my month's notice. He demanded payment for the remaining four months on the lease agreement."

"I can find out about that."

"Fat chance! He's pulled a rent increase without warning. There's total lack of maintenance. Him tearing around on his motorcycle at four a.m.. He said he couldn't *allow* me to move out without paying. Then he buzzed me several times with his bike as I was walking to my car. I was going to come over, but I didn't feel up to people after that. I went to Kmart and sat at the lunch counter until they closed the store."

"You should phone the police," I say. "Do you want me to phone the police?"

"I did. They said they'd have a chat with him. They weren't very convincing."

I raise my knee through the water scum. I want to get out

of the bath and dry off, but I don't know what to do with the phone.

"Come stay with us," I say. "Until you get things straightened out over there." Then selfishly, stupidly, I add, "As long as you like. Hint hint hint hint."

"I can deal with it," she says.

I attempt to lighten my approach. "We get thirty-one channels. All-Science...Nashville...Disney...."

"I know what you have," she says. "I'm not so sure what you want."

"I don't want anything."

"Thanks a lot, Romeo," she says.

I feel set up.

Ignacio is up a tree, legs dangling straddle his branch. I have pruned the trees back so he can't use them to escape the yard. He sees me come out of the house, but doesn't immediately come down. It's cool out this morning and I realize I haven't given much thought to what I'll do with him in winter. House-train him? He places one thick olive leg at a time on a branch, raises himself, then considers his position before starting down. I think of my colleagues who would encourage him to jump.

Most avian theorists agree that *Archaeopteryx*, the oldest known bird, a creature discovered in the one hundred fifty million-year-old Solnhofen limestones in Bavaria, walked bipedally before developing flight apparatus. But they are not willing to consider that it may have taken off from the ground. I picture their early bird, with new bipedal bird-legs and imperfect wings, climbing a tree in order to glide to earth again. It looks preposterous — but I'm sure they envision a more quadradexterous creature.

I have examined numerous photographs of the Berlin specimen of *Archaeopteryx* and, to me, the respective proportions of femur to tibia to metatarsus suggest clearly that this bird-creature was a ground-dweller and a fast runner too.

The skeleton is quite like those of many theropod dinosaurs, quick bipedal predators.

Ig eyes Di as she comes out the door with his mealworms and a few over-ripe blueberries. I look at her doubtfully.

"Balanced breakfast." She grins.

Ig ambles over to us like an arthritic cat. He picks meal-worms from among the blueberries, adeptly flicking the latter off her hand with his tongue. He is a good-looking lizard.

Di coaxes him onto his hind legs by raising his food. He can stand almost erect without support. He takes a step forward.

"What did Lalla say?" asks Di. She squats to watch our lizard chew a blueberry. He pushes it out between his tight lips, blue juice dripping. "Ug, Ig," she says, wiping his mouth with a leaf.

"She didn't say," I say. "I think we should back off. I don't think we should push."

"We're not pushing, we're offering."

"People have to make their own decisions, Di."

"I've mastered that one, Dad," she says.

She stands and examines the berry blotches on her palms. "Look at this," she says. "This one looks like a skull." It does. I try to critically identify the blueberry-stain skull on my daughter's hand, seriously calculating its comparative dimensions. Maybe *Ramapithicus.*

Thursday of the following week, Lalla and I cancel our afternoon classes and make love at my place — twice, she is very tense — and she finally falls asleep while I massage her feet. She has gorgeous feet, small ones with incredibly high arches. She has to have special shoes made because of her arches.

We think we love each other, but timing is everything. "I'm not sure this is the right time for us to make a commit-ment," she's said any number of times. The university is cutting back faculty by eight percent next year and neither of us has tenure. Paleontologists are not in big demand; and what university would want two, a package deal? "And what if they let you go and keep me?" What if. And she doesn't want the bad situation at her apartment building to affect her decision. And she's not certain she's ready to become a mother-figure to an eleven-year-old. I'm not ready for that either, I tell her, but it's cheap entertainment.

There are pink patches on the white sole of Lalla's foot, like quartzite.

Di's mother, Marla, and I had little in common. Except that neither of our families had any money; all four parents worked at lousy jobs for poor wages and raised their children to believe they could be anything they wanted to be. A singer and a paleontologist — maybe they were right. I plan to repeat the experiment with Di. Right now she wants to be a sitcom actress. Marla would flip. "Steer her away from the glamour professions," she said. "See that she gets her sciences, all of them." But one of the last sentences I heard from her was "Don't stifle her creative spirit." The last one was "It's nobody's fault." I still buy that.

If Lalla moves in, I'll probably write Marla care of her agent and suggest divorce proceedings. Though Lalla and I have not once discussed marriage.

"Marry me, you foot," I say softly to her toes, then place the foot gently on the bed and cover it.

She wakes and raises her head off the pillow. She's lying on her stomach and as she rises the sheet slides down her broad back and the constellation of freckles appears.

"Is she home?" she asks, meaning Di. "Should I dress?"

"You're safe," I say.

"How about you?"

"I'm out to microwave a snack. You interested?"

"I'll wait for Di. Leave us something."

I savor every minute with this woman. I know it probably wouldn't be every minute if she moved in, but I can't imagine it otherwise. I want to call and threaten the warlock. I've fantasized about appearing at his door with a fake badge, maybe a toy gun I could pull from a plastic shoulder holster ("Vice! Freeze!"), something to spook him into letting her out of the lease. Di said, "You should eat his lunch, Dad. Go over there and eat his lunch. He's probably a wimp." But I know Di doesn't really expect me to go over and rough the kid up. When I was her age, I expected *my* father to, and I thought less of him when he didn't get physical with people. I apologized for that recently, but he didn't remember these instances. He shrugged, my father who refused to eat anyone's lunch.

"Bipedal carriage preceded evolution of flight machinery," I tell my Friday morning Intro to Vertebrate Paleontology class. "If you walk, or run, on two legs, that frees the other two to do something else. Bipedality releases the forelimbs from the normal business of support and locomotion."

Chuckie, in the third row, sings "C'mon baby, do the Locomotion" every time I use the word, and this is the tenth time this hour. He is still getting laughs, so I don't expect him to give it up just yet. About half the kids in the class are actually interested in the course, and about twenty percent of those are interested this morning. Tough audience.

"What is the smallest known carnivorous dinosaur? Chuck?"

Shrugs.

"Joan?"

"Sorry."

"Anybody?"

"..."

I tell them. "*Compsognathus.* About the size of a modern pigeon. Fossil remains were found in the same Solnhofen limestone that produced all known specimens of *Archaeopteryx.* Despite shorter forelimbs it is very similar to *Archaeopteryx*. And being bipedal and a predator, what do you suppose *Compsognathus* did with its small hands and arms?"

"..."

It's 8:42 Friday morning. I'm asking nineteen-year-olds to speculate on the body functions of a pigeon-sized reptile that has been extinct for at least one hundred million years. Their grey matters stay grey.

"Well?" I ask, "What was there to do in the latter two-thirds of the Mesozoic? Play piano? Hulahoop?" A few snickers, not as many as Chuckie got for his tenth "Do the Locomotion."

Joan, an older student, maybe twenty-three, genuinely interested, searches desperately through her textbook for the answer. I can see she feels she's letting me down.

"Small reptile," I prod, "short forelimbs, sharp teeth. What might he prey upon? Smallest known carnivorous dinosaur. How about insects?"

A confirmation of nods.

"Might he have chased and caught insects? Been not so much carnivorous as insectivorous?"

I draw a crude *Compsognathus* on the chalkboard, intentionally giving the creature tiny arms. Lalla walks Groucholike past the door and gets big laughs from the handful of students who see her. Chuckie can hardly contain himself.

"Some of you will be taking Triassic from Ms. Gilmour next year. If you continue to evolve, you'll be allowed to take my Jurassic course." Stupid teacher joke. No laughs, and the ones who didn't see her have no idea what I'm talking about.

We discuss possible evolutionary improvements for *Compsognathus.*

"Longer forelimbs," guesses Joan, ready to back off if it's not what I want. But it is.

"Right," I say. "And what ways might that happen?"

"Bone growth?"

"Okay."

"Larger hands?"

"Great."

"Longer claws?"

"We're catching insects here, remember."

"A butterfly net," suggests Chuckie.

"Right!" I say. This gets a laugh, but technically it's Chuckie's laugh. "If *Compsognathus*, or his ancestors, could snare leaping insects or bat down flying ones by use of larger forelimb surface areas..." I sketch a few tentative lines on the drawing's tiny arms. "...that would make him more efficient, right?"

General acceptance.

"And what form might that enlargement take?"

"Larger scales?" Joan says — asks. She is a bright young woman. I'm going to invite her to dinner and introduce her to Ignacio. I think she'll like that.

"How about feathers?" I ask the class.

"I'm a woman with an open mind and an educator with an eye to progress," she says, "but what I see and hear these days disturbs me practically to the point of no guaranteed return, Mr. MacDonlaigh, it definitely does."

Pinatel.

"I'm not the meddler you might think I am, nor am I an officious snoop like some on faculty here I could easily mention, but I do regard my students as my daytime charges and you must agree with me when I say that what goes on in their out-of-class lives has direct effect on their in-class behavior and therefore their fellow students and myself as well. So you can understand my concern. Your Di is a dear darling child and deserves a sane stable normal life, and though I'm positive you care deeply and mean well, there are areas where a father, enthusiasm unmodified, can get carried away.

"When I was a girl, Mr. MacDonlaigh — and that was not so long ago as you might imagine, not that I consider myself a young woman anymore, but I keep fit, I have walked many a mile and am still a practitioner of selected RCAF exercises, so

I keep up with my class, don't you worry. When I was a girl, perhaps younger than your own daughter, my parents permitted me to keep a frog. I can see where that bit of information might not shock you, but a frog, in the line of possible pets, I think you will agree with me, is substantially more exotic than a dog or a rabbit or hamster or a Common Bob White housecat. A frog is a creature of the wild, and that is part of its attraction to a young person, you will get no dispute from me there. Had a snake come my way, who knows? I am not afraid of snakes. There is very little I am in fact afraid of — of which I am afraid. I am not afraid of you, for instance. I have, over the years, had to confront a good many parents on a distressing range of topics. But I am afraid, if afraid is the word, for your daughter and daughters like her, any child who is unduly subjected to the deviant quirks of contemporary adult behavior, spousal discord not the least of it. But your marital affairs are none of my business, I want no knowledge of them, it's school policy not to even ask."

Di and Lalla battle the front door with their hips, knees, elbows, heels, their arms filled with bags of groceries. Lalla gives me a strained look like why don't I put the phone down and give them a hand. I point to the receiver and whisper, "P." I raise my eyebrows at Di, and she deposits her bags on the counter, makes a finger pistol with one hand, places the index finger-barrel to the roof of her mouth and pretends to pull the trigger.

"Specifically," says Pinatel, "I must ask you whether or not this horror show lizard exists. I will not, though most would, jump to the automatic conclusion that photographic evidence is evidence enough. Do you or do you not keep this creature in your home?"

"We have a Banded Basilisk." Lalla winces sympathetically at Di, then faces me and does her lizard tongue thing.

"Do you honestly think it wise to subject a child to such extremes of nature, such —"

''For research purposes.''

''Research,'' she says. Pause. ''Research. I will not pry as to what manner of research you might possibly be carrying on with an animal the like of that. That too is none of my business. My business is the education and well-being of my students. But I must point out to you, in good conscience, that research has also shown us that many single parents attempt to conciliate their children with pets following the loss of the other — relocated — parent. We are told that the animal is, or plays the role of, a surrogate!''

There is, strangely, a level upon which I appreciate her concern for my daughter. But.

''Mrs. Pinatel,'' I say, ''I really appreciate your concern.''

''...surrogate mothers, sexual surrogates, test-tube babies, in*vee*tro fertilization, sperm donors, abortions, adoptions, Big Brothers, weekend parents, Parents Without Partners...''

''My concern,'' I continue, ''as yours, I'm sure, is simply the raising of a healthy, well-adjusted, well-educated, optimistic human being.''

On that note Lalla pulls Di to her and they hug each other theatrically. I want to bail out of this and dive between them. After a few seconds Lalla holds Di at arm-length and says, ''Daddy's optimistic human being.''

Di takes the phone. ''Hi, Mrs. Pinatel,'' she says cheerily. ''It's Di. Dad had to go fix dinner.'' She describes a meal she herself would not eat but which includes at least two items from each major food group, then starts in about firing ceramic beads in the school kiln. She's taken control.

I mix up a large can of peeled tomatoes and a can of tomato paste, chop big chunks of assorted vegetables for a spaghetti sauce. I can see Lalla through the kitchen window. She is pacing slowly down the yard alongside Ignacio, letting him choose his speed, and she appears to be talking to him. I lift the sliding storm window and try to listen in, but I only catch her high notes. When Ig stops, she stops. She sits beside him, and soon he's lying across her lap, being stroked between his shoulder blades, arching his neck skyward.

Joan arrives. She's wearing dinner-at-the-prof's clothes: a below-the-knee tweed skirt and a cashmere sweater. She hands me a bottle of wine and looks the room over, doing a double-take on Di. I can't remember if I've mentioned my daughter to her.

"Nice place," she says. "I expected more museumlike. You know, Mesozoic reptile skeletons, and like that."

"We're classic Jurassic here," says Di, just off the phone and hurrying over to meet Joan. She does a weird educational-film voice: "Reptiles still dominate the land."

Joan says, "Hi, I'm Joan."

"Di," says Di. "Has she met Ig?"

"Not yet. He's in conference with Lalla."

They're gone, Di leading Joan by the arm. I stir the sauce, add some black pepper, another dusting of oregano, and listen to a series of ohmygods from outside and Di's triumphant laughter. I have a look. Lalla is standing with her arms around Di again. The recent increase in physical contact between these two has not escaped my notice. Di is leaning into her trustingly. They're both talking rapidly to Joan and to each other. I step outside with the mealworm can, tapping it with a spoon, and, according to plan, Ignacio rises and heads toward me, building speed. He runs bipedally for about ten yards. I wanted Joan to see this.

"That's wild," she says. "You never told me about this guy."

"House secret," I say, spooning mealworms.

"Almost," says Di.

Lalla pinches my thigh and says, "He won't be once he starts flying around the neighborhood."

"That's right!" says Joan. "You should have him catching his own insects so his forelimb scales will grow and become feathers."

"You've been flapped," says Lalla.

Joan, to my satisfaction, recites, "'From flapping swipes at flying or leaping insects, to flapping leaps up after escaping insects, and, with small evolutionary adaptations, such as improvement of the adductive powers of the pectoral muscles, powered flight, from the ground up.'" She beams.

"The great bug net theory of avian flight," says Lalla. She puts her arm around my waist and hooks a beltloop with her thumb. Her free hand absently fondles Di's hair. Joan smiles at us, not individually but as a unit.

At dinner Lalla tells us about apartments she's looked at — a place one thin wall removed from a woman who runs an illegal daycare, several wanting her to sign three-year-minimum lease agreements, places without windows — no luck. The three of us explain Lalla's situation with her warlock landlord to Joan, who is suitably amused and appalled and tells Lalla about a single-bedroom coming open in her building at the first of the month. I bite my tongue. It sounds nice and there's no lease. Lalla says it's worth a look, but she is without enthusiasm. I take this as a good sign.

Then she says defeatedly, "I think he's got me. Legally or otherwise. I'm just not up to the hassle."

Joan is uncomfortable with Lalla's sudden seriousness. "He's not really a warlock," she assures herself.

"I think he is," says Di. She bugs her eyes, blanks her face, does *Children of the Damned.*

"He's a small-d dink. Pardon me," Lalla says.

I don't know what to say. I don't. We've talked about it and danced around not talking about it for weeks. I shake my head in agreement. I feel defeated too.

Di says to Joan, "I begged her to move in with us. We have a room for her and everything."

Joan carefully elects not to reply.

"The feathers room?" Lalla.

''You peeked,'' I say. But this is better.

''Maybe I was checking out the closet space,'' she teases. ''Actually, I thought I heard bird noises in there. Those are very impressive drawings, Flap.''

Joan laughs, partially from relief.

''Professor MacDonlaigh,'' says Lalla. ''Sorry.''

''Flap?'' asks Joan.

Lalla winks at Joan, Joan winks at Di, and I lean back in my chair, enjoying this, and looking at them, not individually, but as a unit, with some territoriality, some wine-heightened sense of protectiveness and possession.

Around 10:30 I bow out in the middle of a game of Scruples and announce I'm going for tonic water, swirling partially melted ice cubes in my glass as a visual aid. I'm accused of being afraid of revealing my basic wickedness by answering more of the game's questions, asked if I'm off to check the night sky for *Archaeopteryx*, a few other jabs I don't quite catch.

There's not much traffic. People are either at home or already out somewhere for the evening, not on the streets. Six minutes after stepping out my front door, I'm swinging into Lalla's parking slot. There are no names or apartment numbers marked on the curb, but I've never known one tenant to swipe another's spot. Under Geerter, the kid's father, this was a really nice place to live. Di and I once considered renting here, before we found the house and before I met Lalla. Horenson lives here somewhere — or did — his rooms outfitted with medicine masks and ceremonial slipcovers. I briefly consider hunting him up, asking his help, but decide against becoming a faculty lounge story.

There's just enough light from the four wrought-iron lamps to illuminate the sidewalk from the parking lot to the main courtyard. Behind the lamps I know are overgrown shrubs, tall dying grass, aluminum drink cans and motorcycle tracks. I get detailed descriptons, though Lalla banned me from coming over when her troubles first began. It's a wonder to me that the tenants don't band together, mass complain, withhold rent. Maybe the kid has intimidated the right people, maybe they faithfully believe in Geerter's return.

I walk across the main courtyard, past the pool, where half a dozen teenagers are climbing on and falling off of an inflated waterbed mattress. The front office, for some reason, is located in number two courtyard, and I'm heading that direction when I see Boy Landlord standing in the far corner in front of the incinerator, the door open, flames moving thin strips of shadow across his big young face, the rest of him dressed in black. When I get closer I see the cape.

He spins around and I duck instinctively out of the light. I watch him remove a cylindrical object from a bag resting on the ground beside him and throw the object into the incinerator, slamming the door shut and stepping back. "*Chun-chun-weena-bwannow*," he sings, his right hand repeatedly crossing his groin and his left hand fingering the air beside his head. "*Bwannow now!now!now!*" There is a loud explosion and the flames find cracks in the furnace door. He throws it open again and laughs at the fire. I remain crouched, hidden behind nothing but night. He dances from side to side, rocking on slightly bent knees, his cape swishing against his extended buttocks. He's maybe six two and thickly built, but just a kid. I've seen him in daylight, assisting his father, but I can't picture him that way right now. Another explosion.

I stand up and walk the rest of the way over with exaggerated briskness, burning up some of the epinephrine produced by my confrontation anxiety. "*Bwannow chichichichichi....*" This close, I can see his hands imitating a guitar player's. He reaches into his bag. An aerosol can. Sees me coming, looks directly at me, picks up three, pitches them into the fire, and this time doesn't bother to shut the door, just steps to the side, placing the incinerator between us. Three staggered explosions. Flames roll out between us, each burst obscuring him momentarily and causing him to reappear as if walking through the flames. Then it's over and he's standing there not really looking at me. On his black T-shirt is a cartoon of a hooded executioner, with a victim's head tumbling from the chopping block, a confused expression on the face. Written beneath, it says: WANT SOMETHING? JUST AXE.

"Hi," I say.

He jerks a set of orange foam-ended headphones down onto his neck and shakes a finger inside his left ear, examining the wax, then wiping it inside his pants pocket.

"I'm here on behalf of Lalla Gilmour, two forty-six."

"So?"

"Well," I say, "I think it would be better —"

"You her dad?"

"No. No, I'm not."

"Brother?"

"No."

"Lawman?"

"Listen —"

"Just who the fuck are you then, buddy?"

"Listen," I tell him. "If you don't want to fix things around here or maintain the property, that's frankly fine by me, but you can't stop someone from moving out of the building." I go on with my suggestions for fair treatment of tenants and their fair expectations of him. I go on for some time and he lets me. I'm using my modulated instructor's voice. I hate this.

"Get!" he says, pointing toward the parking lot. "Fuck off or lose it, buddy." The kid's chin juts defensively and vibrates, like a palsied Marine.

"I'm making a civil demand."

"Save a whale, buddy. Just march yourself out of my face before I decide to kick the steaming fuck out of you. You hear?"

I say some things about contacting his father...a rentalsman...the police...a city councilwoman I know...about organizing tenants...unpaid rents.... The further I go, the shakier my ground. I can't *do* anything. I live in another part of town. The person I'm arguing for is in no way related to me and has not enlisted my support — the reverse is true. But by now I'm not arguing for her, I'm arguing for me. For what *I* want. What, in my accepted belief, he is keeping from me, by spell or legal contract. Did I say *what?* (Territory, coveted territory, self-owned but fenced in by this....) *Who* not what. Lalla.

Fuckfuckfuck, he says, buddybuddybuddy.

He grabs up a stick and another aerosol can, taps the can lightly, rhythmically with the stick.

"Demand, demand," he says. "Do I look like a goddamned errand boy to you, buddy? Do I look like a fucking joe-fixit maintenance man? Give this some thought: I'm the fucking landlord! I own the place, ignorant bastard! Fly, fuck!"

He pokes his twig in the incinerator's fire, then holds it out and sprays hairspray dregs my direction. Instant flame-thrower. He comes at me like that, Buddy Boy Landlord Warlock, black cape billowing behind — *just a minute!* But I run. I scan apartment windows and balconies for witnesses. No one. I run without pride, my unconditioned legs heavy and aching. Past the pool. "Haul ass!" yells one of the girls. Yes. Hauling my uncooperative ass. "You saw it!" I yell back at her. "Sure did." She laughs. And looking behind me I see he's not there. I fled unchased. MacDonlaigh, 1985: feathers as a means of escape. Why? Did I actually think he would burn me?

But I begin plan two — Plan Pinatel — I open the car door and lift Ignacio from the back seat, thinking of Lalla and, whether she moves in with us or with Joan or with...no matter, I've got to...but holding Ignacio there in front of me, in my trembling hands, shielding myself with this poor creature, planning to frighten the kid into releasing her as he frightened her into this kind of confinement, frighten him with an uncommonly large, displaced lizard who has no understanding of this, no quarrel, no desire or ambition beyond eating and retaining heat. He stares at my mouth. The origin of threatening behavior. But I sense he sees in me no threat. And rightly so: I am no threat, to him or anyone. The splashes in the pool are real. There is no hoodoo, there is no voodoo. "This is a human thing," my nonthreatening lips say to him. "This is the Age of Man." I return to the incinerator, without my lizard, and write Geerter Jr. a cheque to pay out the lease. Immediately, he ceases to exist.

It seems such a long time, but I was only gone an hour. When I pull into the driveway I find the three of them examining the neighbors' lawns with flashlights.

"He's gone!" says Di.

"Got out!" Joan adds. "We went out back and he wasn't there. That's a six-foot fence!"

Lalla looks distressed for me. "God, I'm sorry, Flap. I have no idea how he got out. Where have you been all this time?"

I know that a part of each of them believes he flew.

I carry Ignacio cradled in my arms into the house and sit with him in the swivel rocker.

"Where did you find him?" I hear Joan ask.

Then I get it from Lalla, and as I tell her the truth I get it even more. Joan says something about seeing me in class on Monday, but Di takes her down the hall to her bedroom. She spends the night there. The more I tell the truth, the more I tell the truth; and the more complex the emotions I describe, the simpler my sentences become. A distillation process takes place.

"Move in."

And she does.

DIMINISHING

THIRTY-ONE YEARS AGO Denzel's father was run over by a car and killed instantly. Struck, the patrolman said, struck by an eastbound passenger vehicle while walking along the highway. A police radio sputtered code numbers. Why would he have been walking along the highway so far from town? the patrolman asked Denzel's mother. She surely didn't know. His aunt said she couldn't imagine. And the two women set about cleaning Denzel's father's things out of the house almost immediately. Denzel watched his parents' bed burning in the garden — burned there on his aunt's advice — the November frost melting, dampening the mattress and sending slow rolls of smoke into the air. His mother watched the burning feathers from the porch, showing no emotion. Her new bed was much smaller, with barely enough room for Denzel to sit on its edge on Sunday morning, listening to her read him the funnies and the odd headlines from around the world. His father had been walking along the highway because of his smallness, Denzel knew. His father had been small like him, a slip of a man. His father had accepted his smallness and sought to diminish still further, to go unnoticed. He had been walking out of sight.

I am really growing right now, Denzel's wife said during an

argument, and you just don't seem to want to keep up with me. She was right too. He was being left behind. Caught short — that was it — he'd been caught again. There was certainly that feeling to it, the feeling of being caught, found out, exposed. Everywhere, gawkers gawked, and the rest fondled him like a child. Touching his arm, patting his back, giving his shoulder a squeeze, or easing up on a handshake. Denzel was acutely aware of the largeness around him. He thought of the energy generated from the friction of cloth as his co-workers passed his desk, their huge heads and hands often approaching him in misplaced parental gestures. He was five feet one inch. There were plenty of shorter men, he told himself, but not here, here with all this food, all this space. His own children had outgrown him. (But wasn't that what he wanted for them? Wasn't that why he married Pam, to give his children better genetic odds for size?) Now they treated him much the same way his co-workers did. With fondness, yes, genuine affection, but the wrong kind, a kind rooted in protectiveness, uninvited concern for his safety and comfort. You are *my* children! he wanted to yell.

Denzel's father's death was a tragedy, but not the type to bring with it sustained sorrow, like death from prolonged illness or one family member murdering another. There was no apparent conflict, and the unfortunate incident was passed off as cruel randomness. Denzel hoped here to establish a pattern, like father like son, make them reconsider, give it some thought. That was why he chose the method.

We are well below the norm for this time of year, the radio weatherman said as Denzel pulled into a parking space on the far side of the Howard Johnson's restaurant. Deep, deep in the well below, we are well below the norm. Under the weather. This low looks like it will continue to sit on us for at least the next several days.

But the sun soon broke through the low stratus clouds and

Denzel's neck began to perspire, his shirt absorbing the moisture from his neck and shoulders. Where his shirt did not touch the skin, in the shallow gullies on either side of his spine, slow rivulets formed and flowed toward his waist. His cheek felt surprisingly comfortable on the asphalt, shifting its weight now and then, muscles moving of their own free will against the road, adapting. His entire body so quickly accepted the hard, foreign surface that Denzel felt betrayed. Self-betrayed. His back baked. His chest, stomach and the fronts of his thighs soaked surface warmth from the highway, and he began to enjoy the underlying cool. Two motorcycles took the passing lane, veered wide around him, not so much as slowing to gape, their tight engines tearing by, they would talk about him tonight and create their own stories. Denzel hoped for a big Buick, a big cream-colored Buick. He wet his lips with his tongue and tasted oil, salt, something else, the taste of air an inch above a highway. He had driven this stretch of road a hundred times to examine the precise lay and contour, to find the single most unavoidable spot. A Buick would cruise over the low hill, its driver distracted by the road further ahead, the endless expanse of fields, and it would be too late — perfectly timed.

A coach: Your size is against you, Denzel. Nothing we can do about that.

I am not large enough for life, thought Denzel. How can anyone be large enough for life. Growth, expansion, breaking new ground, getting over, rising above, going beyond, stepping forward, reaching out, speaking up, big man, sitting tall in the saddle, with high hopes, worth their weight in gold, pound for pound the best, fat cat, a leg up, more than ever, we're thinking big.

Buick? Denzel whispered wishfully. Harlan Michaels drove his tractor to the top of the hill and stopped directly above Denzel. He was mowing weeds along the roadside. He shut off the mower but left the tractor running. Denzel waited, not permitting himself to look up, but knowing this was not the sound a Buick made. You okay? shouted Harlan. Fine, said Denzel. Well, what are you doing lying there like that? Minding my own business, said Denzel. You best get off the road, don't you think? Just drive on around me. I can do that, said Harlan, but I really think you should get up and go home. You need a ride? Harlan persisted, even trying to pry the man off the road, until Denzel screamed a long scream and started kicking. Harlan drove around him, leaving a patch of tall grass and weeds unmown. It was a long time before Denzel realized he could no longer hear the tractor. What if he hadn't seen me? Denzel considered. What if he had just mown ahead, blades slashing half-on half-off the highway. I could have been hacked to death. Smaller pieces covering a larger area.

A car approached at high speed. Denzel, longing to be large enough to spread his body across both lanes, uncurled his toes inside his shoes.

Harlan had phoned the police.

The patrolman dragged Denzel off the road by his left wrist and belt. He sat Denzel on the hood of the patrol car, and Denzel sized himself up in the patrolman's mirrored sunglasses. In a quick question and answer session, the patrolman determined that Denzel was all right, just another fool-headed civilian. Don't tell my *why* then, said the patrolman. I don't need to know why. *What* you're doing is illegal and you are under arrest. Denzel's rights were read without enthusiasm and he was helped into the back seat of the patrol car. It was very clean. It smelled of disinfectant. Denzel looked at the patrolman through the wire mesh partition. He is an extraordinarily big man, Denzel observed, now looking beyond him, down the highway toward the horizon. But we are heading for the vanishing point, big man, and I will go first.

TSUNAMI

SOMETHING LIKE SUE, Zeke says. Suez? How's Suez?

Su-*ez*, thinks Suez. Suez, was that it?

What do you think of Suez, Charla?

Sue, thinks Suez. Sue. Why not Sue or Susan or Susannah or Susie? Susie's nice. Endearing but spunky too.

Sussy maybe, Charla suggests. How's Sussy, Zeke? Sussy — or Swoozy! Swoozy's good. Like Swoozy Kurtz. *Swoo*-zy!

She'd have to stand her entire life hip cocked and eyebrow raised. Swoozy, humpf.

Susie, thinks Swoozy.

Zuzu. Here's one. What d'you think of Zuzu, Zeke asks. Zuzu'd give her my Z. I like that. *Zuzuzuzuzuzu*, he coos.

Zuzu, Charla scoffs.

Zuzu's got it in spades over Swoozy, thinks Zuzu. Swoozy! A slow bicycle ride on a hot day.

She'll get Zoo, Charla insists. Zoo, Zeke, believe me.

Zudora, Zeke offers, Zuelia, Zulema, Zulpha, Zuni, Zsusanna, Zsuzsi.

Zsa Zsa, right? Let's skip the Zs, okay. Maybe for a boy, Zeke. Maybe a Z boy's name.

Fine, says Zeke, hurt, fine. Maybe plain jane Susan. Or Sue, for Pete's sake. *Zuzuzuzuzuzu*, he murmurs.

Zuzu, Zuzu agrees. Zuzu, Daddy Papa.

Suez was all right. I wasn't opposed to Suez, Charla says. You weren't *for* it either, were you? No.

I didn't say, did I? I didn't commit myself. No, I didn't.

Which I took to mean you were not at all enamoured.

Which you then took wrongly, Zeke. I'd short-list Suez. Put it down.

Suez! Thought we'd gone by that, thinks Suez. Suez. An Egyptian city. A gulf. A canal. An isthmus. Geography — what if I'm no damn good at geography? Sweet Suez in the dunce's fez. Suez. Why not Sioux City Sue, then? Sault Sainte Marie? Sudan? Hsu-Chou?

Sussex, Sukey, Suki, Sugi? Just nod Yes or No, Zeke. Suzu?

That's what I said just a minute ago, Charla. Zuzu.

Not *Zu*zu, Zeke, *Su*zu. The book says it's Japanese for *little bell.*

What's Zuzu mean?

No such name, Zeke.

She'd be an original.

She'd be Zoo. Believe me.

What were the others you said?

Sussex? Sukey? Suki? Su —

Suki. What's Suki?

Japanese for *beloved*, Miwok Indian for *chicken hawk with a long tail.*

Miwok?

Miwok, Zeke. Here, how's Suletu? Suletu's Miwok for *California jay flying out of a tree*. Or Soso —

Soso!

Soso's Miwok for *tree squirrel biting a tiny hole in a pine nut.*

Zuzu, thinks Soso. Zuzu or Susie or Sue.

Suni, Suri, Sudy, Sutra, Sufi, Sula, Susu...

We're back to Zuzu, Charla.

*Su*zu. And I don't like it anyway.

Fine. *(Zuzuzuzuzuzu.)*
Suela, Sue-Ella, Situla, Sultana, Suzamni?
Suzamni vomits charmingly on Zeke.
Tsunami, says Zeke. Not Suzamni, Tsunami.
She'd get Tsu all the time.
So? She'll always get abbreviated. Kids abbreviate.
Tsu! Tsunami longs to cry out. Cries out instead.
Tsunami, Charla weighs. How's about Naomi, Zeke. You like Naomi?

THE AWAY PLACE

CARLIGHTS ON THE HIGHWAY OUTSIDE pass in aureate orbs across my front curtains. The cars themselves, at such high speeds, make electric shearing sounds.

I always attempt to relax myself before my client arrives, to prepare, but the knock at my door never fails to excite me. I have told Rosa Coover that it is important for me to relax in her presence, that it is part of the process. She claims she too appreciates the time to settle herself and focus her energy. We spend some time being silent together. We talk very little before or after our sessions.

''Should we begin?'' I ask when I know we're both calmed.

I have seated myself on the small significant-looking rug. Rosa is in the client chair. Many of them feel they should join me on the floor. They worry about levels. The levels they mean are the altitudes of horizontal surfaces. These do not concern us, I tell them.

''I believe I'm ready,'' she says.

Rosa is a young woman, perhaps ten years younger than myself, in her early thirties, prettier too, tall and narrow-hipped, but generally anxious. I always picture a young family waiting outside for her in a station wagon — two clean children, a broad-faced husband in a necktie — though I know she comes alone and leaves in a taxi.

Twice a week, for the past five weeks, we have summoned Everett. I am uncertain who Everett is. Unlike most clients, Rosa offered no information, no family history, no anecdotes concerning the spirit (I ask for none, but most gladly tell me their stories). I do not require knowledge of their past relationship to perform the transmission.

While in my trance I hear only confusing pieces of the spirit's speech, and, passing through me, the voice is contained within my own limited range. The human voice can warp bizarrely, but the voice is always recognizably my own. It is one measure of authenticity in a medium: that the medium's voice duplicates the spirit's within her given vocal boundaries. But I lose the sound of my client's voice in the process; I lose external hearing.

Once contact is secured, it is only my physical self which is necessary for transmission. My mind makes the connection, and then I can leave by following the blue line. I can go to the away place.

My greatgrandmother Wimona Cordelia Sissell, who recognized in me her own "condition" and knew how it would soon govern my life, spoke of the away place as though it was a holiday resort.

"You'll want to go there about as often as you can," she said, holding me close, her bird-boned hands pressing my ear to her bosom; one ear tuned to her heartbeat, her breath, her inner workings, while the other took in her strange talk, talk I knew she only talked to me, her "sensitive one."

"Your retreat," she said. "Your own island. Like nothing else there ever was."

She always smelled of lavender. When she entered my mother's house I knew instantly. It wasn't a chemical store-scent, but a true flower lavender that charged the air. Pressed against her, deep in it, the fragrance covered me like a mosquito net, a hazy protective seal.

"Is it far?"

She rocked me and sighed. "Not far, darling. Not far at all. Don't you fret, you'll go there soon."

"You too?"

She laughed and said, "I do believe I'm there most of the time these days." She rubbed her lips over my hair. "It's fine," she said. "It's sheer calm. Nobody bothering you. No hurry to go nowhere."

She practiced as a medium until the age of one hundred and four. There was no swinging sign from the arch of her porch entrance. She wasn't to be found in the telephone directory or in newspaper personal ads. People who needed her found her. She called her clients "visitors," and she had visitors almost every day. I'd be left with her while my parents went off somewhere alone, and she'd tell me about her visitors. "This fellow lost his twin in a drunk-driving accident," she'd say. "I think they talk mostly about school days." Or, "Mrs. Thorne lost a little girl about your age. She says she'd have taken her own life if we hadn't made contact." One of her visitors tried for months to contact Houdini, but was entirely unsuccessful. "There has to be a special bond between people for it to work," she said. "I told him that. I told him that right from the start." I watched her sessions from behind the piano; she showed me where to hide.

"I do the little I can," she said. "Sometimes I knock a bit off if I see they've heard a sad thing. But you charge them, darling. You charge them a fair price. It may all seem a natural enough function to you, but it's a service you're providing. A luxury — yes, a luxury, a second chance."

I wasn't sure what it was I was supposed to charge for, but I understood that we had a secret and that too many questions would sap its mystery. I could see she didn't need my questions.

"You understand luxury, don't you?"

I nodded "yes" against her chest, releasing a fresh flow of

scent.

"Sure," she said. She thought a few seconds, then continued, "Maybe this what we have is a luxury. Do you think? Most live just fine without it. But when I was younger I think I sorely needed it. It made some sense of things. It was no end of comfort to me knowing I was necessary and appreciated both here and in the hereafter."

I felt her shrinking away from me. Melting.

"Wait till you feel that big white sun on you," she said. "It's like nothing else."

Rosa sits completely still in the client chair in the northeast corner of the room, concentrating on her memories of Everett.

I enter.

I take the headache from my head and place it in my hand, causing it to swell slightly and throb. My eyes close and my head rolls forward.

"Ruku," I breathe.

The three spirits I must first assemble before finding Ruku have no visual image. I know them by their effects on my body.

The Natural spirit is in my liver. I am in my liver. A great chemical alteration is made by the secreted vapors. It is not painful but uncomfortable caught in the thick steam.

"Ruku."

When my liver begins to cool I approach the Vital spirit in my physical heart. A Freonlike substance runs outward through my veins, as though I am being embalmed by a cryogen, slowly frozen from the inside.

The Animal spirit rises in my brain and wakes my muscles. I feel each individual muscle group activate independently, stretching and contracting, pressing new warmth around my veins, generating enough heat to modify the Vital spirit and reactivate the Natural spirit.

"Ruku."

As the three reach their balance, stasis, I experience the

thawing sensation, a warm fluid downward flow — of what? I snap my neck back severely, setting off the series of flashes. White. Red. A return to black. The white again, becoming whiter, and Ruku, my spirit guide, appears. It is at this point that Rosa can summon Everett. Her instructions are to wait ten seconds after the snapping motion, then say, "Ruku, I must speak with man Everett in this place."

Rosa cannot hear Ruku's voice, though I can, clearly. It is unidentifiably foreign, using clumsy English. His is the only voice I hear which is not my own. (Sometimes the spirit speaks directly to me, knowing I cannot reply while it possesses my tongue.)

Ruku dislikes Everett. He dislikes many spirits.

"He bad dead," I hear him say as he returns through the white.

The transmission begins. The outer surface of my skin pulls, prickles. It marks the arrival of the spirit.

"Man Evett," says Ruku.

Ruku is thin and dark-skinned, but not black, with squinted eyes, as though he is in pain or myopic. And he is naked, but apparently without genitals, completely hairless too. He is male in voice and posture. I often want to ask him questions: about himself, about *them* — but that is impossible. He comes only to perform his duty, then returns, disappears into the white. Once he has brought the spirit, as now, it is too late for me to speak. He may say something, but it is invariably to himself rather than to me.

The formless Everett settles in. Ruku scans above and around him, where Everett must be. Can Ruku see him? Does the spirit have form to the spirit guide?

"You speak today, man Evett?" tiny Ruku asks.

And my masculine Everett voice replies impatiently, "The moment she leaves."

"Touchy dead," mutters Ruku.

I find the faint blue line leading into the upper-left corner of the otherwise pure white (*air*), and I follow it away. What goes on between my client and the spirit is not my business; I am paid to temporarily vacate myself. So I do.

"Will you be going?" Everett asks behind me.

"She gone," says Ruku.

"You!"

In the distance Ruku remarks, "Ain' he the dead to beat all dead."

Being away is the next best thing to being there. Where? *There*: everywhere but here, the location of my physical self. Perhaps being away is better than being here.

The away place is vast and warm and white and silent. It is like nothing else. What I see here is what I project: Wimona Cordelia Sissell standing in the midst of scurrying women in bright flower-print frocks, lots of primary colors. A picnic. The annual family picnic. Our one family taking over the small public park. Picnic benches stained fresh every four years by the Boy Scouts. Boy Scouts in their boy-blue shirts and yellow neckerchiefs and merit badges. Cubs! It's Cubs I'm thinking of. With Den Mothers. My mother, though she had only daughters, was a Den Mother for many years. She thought each young boy held the fate of the world in his hands. She wanted to see them set right to start with. There was no discussion as to the relative value of girls. Girls were at life's mercy, I gathered.

My mother's brother Jonah was shot in a convenience store hold-up by two young men, who were never caught. He lay dying in the hospital for days, in terrible pain, while police repeatedly questioned him about the robbers. I remember hearing him yell at the questioning officer, "Well, they damn well weren't Boy Scouts!" And for years afterward I fantasized that my mother's Cubs had committed the crimes I read about in the newspaper.

A blue border of Cubs surrounds the city park, protecting our family, four generations in attendance, each of us more vivid than in real life.

I was not shown the way and given the key. Greatgrand-mother Sissell died too soon. Ruku first appeared to me when I was fifteen. I was coring apples in the kitchen, alone and daydreaming, when he came into my mind.

"Hallo," he said. He spoke as though annoyed, as though he had been interrupted. It is his normal demeanor.

"Who are you?"

"You sprit guy. You call Ruku."

"Ruku."

"That right. What you want?"

I knew instantly what he meant. I understood what was possible. I bloomed eight shades of red.

"Nothing," I said. "Ruku. Ruku. I — "

"Aye-aye-aye-aye!" he sang sarcastically. "I go then."

He filled his cheeks with air, blew his face up huge like Dizzy Gillespie playing horn, and released the air slowly, turned and disappeared into the white.

A week after his appearance, his introduction, a woman I recognized as one of the cafeteria workers from school stopped me on the street downtown and asked me to contact her brother. And I knew what she meant. Contact. I knew it was something I was now able to do, though I had not attempted transmission before, nor had I been instructed how to do so. I had only watched from behind a piano leg.

We went to her home, drank chamomile tea and talked about her brother, then I informed her I was ready. I cleared my mind of outside images, dispelled the unfamiliar sounds and odors of the woman's house, and called into myself for Ruku. I passed through the three spirits for the first time, in awe and wonder and fear of causing my own death — what was I doing to my body? what damage? I wanted both to turn back and to go deeper. My head — I felt it — rolled back on my shoulders, became heavy, and empty, became a thick-walled chamber, then vanished from my awareness entirely, leaving an open sensation. And Ruku arrived, his pouting self, to fetch my client's brother. It worked! It worked. I was able to maintain transmission for only a few minutes, but it had worked.

Part of the reason for the abbreviated transmission, I think, was my naive fear of the away place. I refused to let myself go, to take myself there. I tried to stay close to the contact point — to keep one foot in the door, I suppose. If I was to follow the blue line, I wanted it to be tangible, something I could hold on to and something I could be certain would be there to guide me back. But it was something I could not touch. I tried to grasp it mentally, but it, like the white, was impalpable, was...ether? I did not want to rely on something over which I had no control, so I moved off in other directions. But I did not seem to move at all. The white was all around me and the blue line remained in its position.

Still, my first client was pleased with my effort. I apologized. I knew I hadn't done a good job for her.

"That's all right," she said, squeezing my arm. "It has been a long time since I talked to that boy, and it was just fine. I thank you for the both of us."

I grinned uncontrollably, felt the newness of my body.

"I'd like us to visit again in a couple of weeks," she said. "Would that suit?" And she handed me three dollars. I accepted it. (Three dollars! The fee is sixty now.)

To my knowledge Greatgrandmother was never asked by anyone in our family how she supported herself. But I cannot believe they knew.

Through my twenties I held a series of low-paying restaurant jobs. I knew I could make do without the extra money, but I felt the need to keep my mediumship a secret from my family — I knew they would ask *me* about money.

It is easier now I live a thousand miles from my nearest relative. But I have a cover: I told them I work as a telephone solicitor out of my home. If one of them comes to visit, I pretend to make a couple of calls — long-life lightbulbs, that sort of thing. To advise my clients in the event of an unannounced family visit, I place a vase of dried flowers in my front window.

Rosa and Everett have been at it a long time. Transmissions typically run forty to sixty minutes. If transmission goes on too long, I rely on the Animal spirit to intervene, to protect me from the strain of prolonged high metabolic activity. I project the image of Rosa. She is walking along the border of Cubs, on the edge of the park, pinning badges on their uniforms and kissing their cheeks. When she has awarded them all, they turn en masse to face my family. They begin to close ranks, to march inward, and I stop the projection.

Moving along the blue line is like sitting in a chair and allowing your eyes to follow a seam up the wall. There is the sense of elevation, of actually moving, rising, of leaving the contact point, but I am not sure whether I really do move or whether it is simply an illusion — my entering a deeper state of consciousness by concentrating on points farther and farther up the line.

I have read books on mediumship and parapsychology, but nowhere have I found a description of my process.

The blue line is fine and faint, and it ends at the away place. There is no end as in cut-off point — it appears to continue on, but following it will take me no further. I trust the line now, without question; I have for years. I look forward to my journeys there — *here*. What I see, as I have mentioned, is what I project, and what I project is a mixture of memory, insight and wishful thinking.

At this moment that is Wimona Cordelia Sissell's death.

I was seven at the time. My mother came to my bedroom and brought me gently from sleep, stroking my hair. "Honey," she said, "Greygrandma's passed away." Away, I thought, away was where she longed to be. "We're all going to miss her an awful lot," Mother said. "But she had a good, long life, and now she's going to her reward." In my projection I see Greatgrandmother accepting an over-sized cheque from a saint and shaking his hand. The whole thing has a game show look about it, but it is a satisfying image: Wimona's payday.

I did not grieve her death. But about a month after her burial I tried to dig her up again. I walked to the cemetery one Saturday afternoon when I was supposed to be at a movie matinee, and I located her monument and began slowly to dig, first with my hands, then with a stick. But I could not move all that moist, rich earth. I had only dug a two-foot square hole when my arms and back became too weak to continue. I don't know who filled it in again — the groundskeeper? one of the family? — but it was filled and tamped the next morning when we all went following Sunday service. I remember, at some point, trying to shove my hand through the bottom of the hole, clawing with my fingertips, trying to reach her casket — her body? I don't know. I don't know what I was trying to do. Did I expect her to reach up and grasp my hand? Just to touch? Did I want to pull her back into this world again? Or for her to pull me into hers? I don't know. But it was not a desperate act, and there was no trace of anger in me. I held no one responsible for taking her away. I saw it clearly as her choice. And I still do.

"Save your love for the living," she advised me once, when I asked her if she still loved Greatgrandfather even though he'd been dead for thirty years. "I love his memory," she said. "But do I love him? How do I know what he's like now, after all this time? I shall see when the time comes."

She held her hand under the lamplight beside her chair and examined the loose, translucent skin. Her veins might as well have been on the outside, they were so visible, even the movement of blood.

"Even you and me," she went on, "there's not much we can do for our loved ones once they're gone. Love the living, the dead will wait."

Ruku has entered the away place. Unusual behavior for him. He remains distant but in view, and he appears to be teetering side to side, his upper body jerks like a chicken's neck. He stands there for a long while, then finally makes his way toward me. Can he see me? Does he always see me? I want to shout to him, invite him nearer, welcome him, but my tongue is still held by Everett. How long? I wonder.

"Lissen," says Ruku. "I tell you somethin. What you know?" He is hugging himself tightly around the chest. "What you know man Evett? What? His lady fran? What you know?" His haggard face comes forward and I see him with a fish-eye lens effect.

"I lissen," he says. "Who boyo boy!" He rolls his eyes and cocks his head.

I wish he would stand still. I wish he'd be his usual lazy, moaning self.

Then he leaves abruptly. "Hang on," he says. Or "I gone." "Agony"? Who knows? Cuckoo Ruku.

When he finally reappears far down the blue line, I am projecting myself. He motions to me, but I am reluctant to go to him. In the projection I am underwater. Immersion. Baptism. Sustained weightlessness. I drift. What does he want?

"Come now," I hear him say hushed but emphatically. I give up my life underwater and go to his aid.

"You lack this place?" he says. "You best lack it. What *I* do now, I'm thinking."

We creep down the blue line together — me unable to ask questions, Ruku offering no explanation.

"Come as close as you like," Everett's voice speaks through my mouth. I was observing Ruku's curious behavior and hadn't realized we were so near the contact point.

"Step right up!" Everett calls, imitating a carney barker. "Step right this way! Don't keep us waiting, the show is about to begin!" He laughs at himself.

Rosa must hear him, so she knows I've interrupted. What must she think of me? A meddler, no doubt. A busybody. But if she is saying anything to Everett, he is ignoring her; he seems bent on tormenting Ruku and I.

"At a loss for words?" he asks. "The cad got your tongue?" He laughs uproariously. "Is that what you're thinking, woman?"

I know I should return to the away place immediately. I have no business being here. But there is no reason for him to taunt me. Ruku is right to dislike this one. Surely Rosa will make him stop. He is wasting precious transmission time with this foolishness.

"Don't be afraid to speak your mind!"

"Mine yourself," says Ruku disgustedly.

"Now, now," Everett condescends. "You know, for a spirit guide, you speak much too freely — for a creature who only holds a visitor's pass in both worlds. Yes, you are tiresome."

Ruku cowers, eyes flashing suspiciously around.

Rosa, please ask him to stop. I can't bring myself to leave while Everett is abusing Ruku, though there is nothing I can do about it. It is disturbing to hear my own voice, no matter how distorted, being so rude.

"What shall I do with you, Ruku?"

"Not you sprit guy. Not you."

"Then whose?"

I am suddenly aware of my body. Transmission continues, but.... There is a jarring, a struggle for balance, a distant untangling of limbs, all unfamiliar, disproportionate....

I am standing! Though I feel as though I'm clinging to the top of a swaying tower.

"Forgive my awkwardness, dear," says Everett. "Your body is so unlike my own. Not just that it's a woman's, but did you know I was better than six and a half feet tall? Yes! I was always very proud of my height. Rosa loves tall men. Don't you, Rosa. I've lost more than a foot in the bargain here. But you're not so old as the others, and Rosa rather likes you. That's important."

What is he doing with me? I feel violated. I want to protest but cannot speak. Somewhere below me I sense my swinging sleeping limbs. He has stood me up and set me walking without disturbing transmission, without my knowledge or participation!

"No," says Everett, "you haven't given me much height."

Given you! I am walking — being walked. Ruku has started up the blue line without me. He looks as though he is hyperventilating. But what can I do for him? This is ridiculous. Everett has gone too far. It is a wonder, to my mind, Rosa hasn't intervened, sent him back.

I seek the Animal spirit to return me.

Weakened red tints the white, but there is no rise in temperature, and the red soon fades. I look to Ruku for help and find him sitting on the blue line with his cheeks distended, blowing staccato whistles.

"Rosa," Everett says, paying no attention to my attempts, "will you find me a coat from this woman's closet, please?"

I concentrate completely. I try to reenter my body by focusing on my pulse, on my heart, on the surge of blood, but I am too far removed, and am held in the white by Everett's presence.

I hear him speak — *myself* speak — casually to Rosa about the time of year, an outdoor market across town, how he has missed taste, then about money: how much, whether it would be theft. "Yes," he says, "does it matter? I see your point!" He laughs again. "How right you are! How right you were about everything!"

"But that coat," he complains. "Isn't there something less feminine? Remember who I am, love."

"Body snatch," says Ruku, his breathing almost returned to normal.

"Unlimited transmission, maybe?" offers Everett. "Indefinite lease? But yes, Ruku, I have decided to stay. Try to make me feel more welcome, won't you?"

He can't do this to me! Can he? Ruku? It occurs to me, with great distress, that I don't *know* precisely what he can and cannot do. I hadn't considered the possibility. I always accepted our respective roles. I —

"What to do?" Ruku asks. Asks me.

"What you like," replies Everett. "I have no use for you. There will be no further transmissions, my dear deposed woman, so you may do as you wish. You may remain here and hang on my every word, or go off somewhere and amuse yourself. I'm not bothered what you do. And Ruku, what to do? You'll soon get used to an eternity with nothing to do. Trot along, might as well get started."

Is it more white? Is it something at the end of a tunnel? (I should know more, you would think, wouldn't you? But what do I really know?) I know the dead. I make my living from the dead. But death? How it looks and feels, what it is? Am I dead now? At this moment? Did I cease living the moment Everett chose to remain in my body? Why didn't the Animal spirit bring me back? Because it saw my body as functional under Everett's control? That's all I can make of it. Is it only concerned with chemical actions and motor responses? Does it maintain no allegiance to me? I don't know the answers. I'm a tabloid headline: **WOMAN LOSES LIFE TO DEAD MAN.**

If I were clairvoyant I'd have seen it coming.

I am waiting out eternity at the away place. I have not seen Ruku in days? weeks? longer? Weeks, I think, but I have no gauge of time here. I feel some hostility toward him, I feel deserted, but why should he stay?

There is no argument about whether or not Everett can do this; it's done; he is a squatter in my body. I don't know if I am, for all intents and purposes, dead, or if I live in limbo and die when Everett — Everett is *already* dead! Do we both die at the end of *my* natural life? Natural life! Is my continued state of being and my body's well-being dependent on Everett's treatment of me? And what sort of life does my body have now? Are they — we — residing in my house, or do I live with Rosa? Do we make love? Man through woman with woman? I no longer believe in Rosa and her station wagon full of family. But maybe, maybe they do exist and we have fled the city to escape them. I have no idea where I am; I have no idea what he is doing with me. I am waiting out eternity in the away place.

The away place is like nothing else. It is vast and warm and white and silent. What I see here is what I project. But it is no longer a sanctum; it is part of my exile and confinement.

I project my parents driving out for a summer visit. My sister Florence at the wheel. Them finding me home all right, but me being Everett being me. And in my projection he pulls off the charade perfectly and they just enjoy him to no end, and his new lodger, Rosa, too. I don't know how the masculine qualities of my speech are explained; it is only a projection.

My projections, endless projections, have begun to lack optimism.

I projected myself coming alive after my burial.

I projected Everett tricking my clients out of their life-savings.

I projected my life underwater again. But this time I was unable to surface at will. Even in my projection.

I tried to project Rosa and Everett, to see them together, but Everett appeared as a bad composite from a Harlequin romance novel.

I do not believe we go to our away place when we die. This is not death. I decided that just now.

Several hundred projections later I hear an ecstatic "Hallo!"

Ruku. I'd resigned myself to the probability of never seeing him again. He is excited, not at all himself. He jigs, hopping from one foot to the other, waving his scrawny arms like bug legs.

"Damn be dead man Evett!"

He pats his cheeks with both hands and makes a whooping noise. Everett cannot help but know he is here, but Ruku doesn't seem to care.

"Ruku do him!" he says. "Come now!" He starts down the blue line.

I am glad he has come back. I want to tell him how glad I am. I also want to tell him how much he upset me by leaving without a word, not a word.

"I guy the sprit for you!" he shouts.

I have no desire to encounter Everett again, to be reminded that I can say nothing, do nothing, to have my helplessness mocked.

But Ruku is adamant: "Now! Come now! I guy the sprit! Evett wild mad!"

Evett wild mad? Has Rosa left him? That would be just the thing. Anything. Something tragic has happened out there and Everett is unable to deal with it.

I follow Ruku anxiously down the blue line toward the contact point, toward Everett, wild mad Evett. We haven't gone far when I hear the voice.

"No! I will not! ...*the worst kind of man* ...I have chosen... *You, sir, are touched*... Yes, touch. Do you remember it?"

He sounds panicky all right.

Ruku halts me well short of the contact point, but the voice is loud and carries clearly, swirling through the white in intense gusts.

"*The dead*... Whose rules? Whose laws? ... *They have lives of their own* ... Just so. Mine is here."

"*I think not.*"

Wild mad. The voice rises and falls, in pitch and volume, debating itself rabidly.

"I will do as I elect to do!" states Everett. Then, in a higher range, "*You are a greedy, foolish soul. You shall know no peace.*"

Ruku drums on his kneecaps.

"I have known no peace. I have made my own."

"*You are losing control, you know that.*"

"Rosa, stay here. You and I —"

"*Losing.*"

"Don't challenge me... *You know, don't you? You can't hold on* ... Rosa, it's only ... *The more you participate out there, the more you lose your hold here. You feel the loss.*"

"Geegeema," says Ruku.

Wimona Cordelia Sissell from my own lips!

How can they both transmit through me at once? Ruku and I listen to the two of them arguing. We are rapt eavesdroppers. Everett refuses to leave Rosa and return to the dead; Greatgrandmother wears away at him with a lengthy sermon on the order of things, threatening divine reprimand and forced removal, threatening him with spatial and elemental concepts I cannot begin to comprehend, until Everett's angry interjections dissipate, and I hear her say, in sole control of my tongue, "Rosa, you will die soon enough. The dead will wait."

Rosa must fear the repercussions from her role as accomplice.

Greatgrandmother laughs. "And what do you imagine I might do to you, child? Did your man talk to you of our special powers? Or do you think I'll have them lock the gates when you die and keep you out?" She laughs again. A tired, affectionate laugh. "Dear girl, there is no power nor want of power here — your Everett perhaps the exception. Go love the living, your dead man will wait."

Then she thanks Ruku and sends him politely on his way.

She talks to me until the white sparks with the scent of fresh lavender and I am assured of natural balance and my fortunate position therein, and she asks, when I am wholly settled, "Would you mind awfully if I stayed a while?" And I am so glad to have her with me again.

In the summer, my family visits, my sister Florence at the wheel. And Wimona Cordelia Sissell feeds them fine meals from both our hearts. They are so glad to be with me again.

RECENT MUSIC

I DON'T KNOW just exactly why I let him in. He had what sounded like a password, maybe that was it. I cracked open the apartment door enough to get a look at him, and he bent forward his ice axe of a nose and said, conspiratorially, "Carpets."

"Carpets," I whispered.

It wasn't his looks. I didn't like the looks of him. He was big, with huge sloping shoulders and a massive bovine chest, and his silver coveralls were too small, pulling up short of his red nylon socks. There was a full two inches or more of smooth, hairless white flesh gaping between his pant legs and those socks. Across a single breast pocket the name "Wendell" was embroidered in a shaky, home-sewn script.

"Carpets," I whispered again, watching my hands unlatch the protector chain and fling the door open wide.

He towed a knee-high chrome unit behind him as he entered. It had a see-through amber bubble on top and a long black hose by which he pulled the thing around.

"No halls," he said.

"Okay."

"No bedrooms. Guy'll be along tomorrow with a smaller machine for those. Saugenmeister 410. You ever seen one?"

"No."

"Incredible little machines."

I just kept quiet.

"Anyway," Wendell continued, "He'll be along tomorrow early."

"I see."

"Elvin."

"Pardon?"

"Guy's name's Elvin."

"Fine," I said.

"Just so you know."

He appeared to be looking directly to the left of my head as he spoke, so I stepped to one side, allowing him full view of the living room carpet. There were a few mysterious stains and it was slightly faded, but it was free of burn holes and paint spots. I felt almost proud. He chewed at a corner of his mouth and closed his eyes tight a few seconds.

We'd moved in a week early because the previous tenants had already moved out, and we managed to persuade the landlord, saying how we wanted to get in and settled as soon as possible, and how the people who bought our house weren't scheduled to take possession yet but had nonetheless begun putting up new siding. As a result, we'd been forced to endure constant interruptions by apartment maintenance people: a plumber, a woman with lightbulbs, a window cleaner, a man to take crayon marks off one of the bedroom walls. "Kids," he'd said, like it was detective work.

That was three weeks ago. We assumed they'd all come who were coming. We'd positioned the furniture how we wanted it and restocked the end tables with their collected miscellany.

"All gotta be moved," pronounced Wendell, coming out of his meditation.

"Couldn't we just shift it to one side?" I asked.

Negative.

As he dragged his carpet shampooer into the kitchen, something leaped into my peripheral vision. Eleanor. Eleanor stood nude in the hallway, half-asleep. Stood there like a wrinkled flamingo, rubbing her right foot against the inside of her left leg. I signalled exaggeratedly for her to get back in the bedroom. She held up a toothbrush.

"Now now now now now," said Wendell, surveying the room.

Her modest breasts went ways of their own as she pivoted and slipped back into safety.

Wendell and I commenced shoving furniture into the hallway. It occurred to me to suggest to Eleanor that she get dressed and come out instead of allowing herself to be blockaded in the bedroom for a couple of hours, but our visitor placed the heavy love seat squarely in front of the door, then stacked a coffee table and footstool on top of that.

"Plug," he said, hands on his big hips and eyes scouting the baseboard of the empty room with a slow careful sweep.

"There," I said, pointing to an outlet beneath the living room window and partially hidden by the curtains.

He handed me the plug and began filling his old chrome shampooer with blue fluid from a root beer jug, absently dripping on his foot.

The machine fired up, emitting a high rotating whine, as I plugged it in. He threw himself backwards and slapped off the toggle switch.

"Loud," he said, grinning.

I fully expected Eleanor to be pounding down the bedroom door, wanting to know what precisely was going on. But she wasn't. All that furniture was probably soundproofing the hallway.

I thought seriously about making myself some breakfast, before I realized I would have to eat standing up. That didn't seem healthy. I couldn't think of anyone who ate standing up. Instead, I leaned against a stack of dining chairs and attempted to recreate the image of my sixty-nine-year-old flamingo-imitating wife. A rosy-white blur.

Wendell waltzed around the living room in tight steps with his incessantly whirring shampooer, working lather circles into larger lather squares. The overhead light reflecting off his high unlined forehead made him appear to be visibly balding.

"It'll take some time," he said.

"No problem," I replied.

"Forgive the inconvenience."

"That's all right."

"You just go ahead with whatever you normally do."

"I've got plenty of time."

"That a fact?"

"I've nothing planned."

"Your day off, is it?"

"Retired," I said, and watched his facial muscles do a dance. The word still felt strange in my mouth — like I knew it was the correct answer but had no idea what it meant.

"Oh?"

"Afraid so."

"Part of the swelling ranks of mature individuals," said Wendell, staring intensely at the rug. "The country's most wasted resource," he said.

"I thought I'd try it for a year or two," I said.

"Retirement," he said, putting some weight on his machine as he approached a dark spot. "Now this is an area about which I am very curious."

"It's all still new to me," I said.

The low double-window in the dining room was open, and the growing clamor of cars and people below on Grant Avenue rose to join Wendell's machine. Traffic and voices tuning themselves. Rounded then stammered vowels, hissing and pipping consonants. Blurts. Wheezes. Saxophones.

"Ours is an ungrateful society," the big man confessed.

"Not at all," I said.

"I don't for one minute blame you retireds for being disenchanted with the system. No, I don't."

"I think I'll like it fine."

"Man like yourself — I suspect differently."

"Best to view it as an extended vacation, I think."

"Vacation," said Wendell. "Is that what you think? If you mean being forced to vacate your hard-earned position at a time of peak mental maturity."

"It was my choice," I said.

Wendell stood up straight as his great body would allow and completely ignoring the rising froth from his stationary machine, said, "I *am* sorry."

His eyebrows floated around his expanse of forehead. He rolled his silver shoulders. "I *am* sorry," he repeated.

Eleanor would have put him back on track, told him to keep to his own side of the fence, but I didn't want to stir him any further.

"A man's daily work must be recognized and appreciated," Wendell explained. "If it isn't, he winds up feeling inadequate, inconsequential, ineffectual. And he gives up. He retires."

"I —" I said.

"I've seen it happen to too many people," he continued. "My own uncle checked himself in and let senium praecox have at him. Now that's voluntary retirement for you."

"Senium praecox?"

"Premature senility. Pick's disease got him, they said."

"I'm sorry to hear that."

"*I'm* sorry," insisted Wendell. "Both as a nephew and as a tithing member of the blessed world community, I'm sorry. If my uncle had enjoyed the occasional scrap of praise while he was working, I truly believe he'd be alive, sane, and toiling his tail off today."

"Perhaps if he'd had a hobby....," I said.

"Hobbies won't keep a man alive. He was a philatelist, a philumenist, and shrewd as a Philadelphia lawyer where chess was concerned. I say you have to have a purpose. A mission, if you will. A man must have a calling."

Saxophones honked in the window like defensive geese, like offensive tenors. A street sweeper drove slowly by, making his brush-against-cymbal percussion clash with Wendell's shampooer's whirr. Eleanor, my Eleanor. You might be calling me this moment and I'd not hear a peep.

"Depression," said Wendell.

"Pardon?"

"Depression," he repeated, his back doing a serpentine movement as he returned to serious cleaning, push-pulling the large chrome unit, moving his soap in advanced geometric variations. "Depression is where it generally starts for most retireds. A lowering of overall mood-tone, feelings of dejection, difficulty focusing their thoughts, that sort of thing."

I walked over to the dining room window not having a clue.

"You and your uncle must have been close," I said, sitting on the windowsill.

The warm wood breathed through my pajama bottoms. Three stories down and across Grant, a woman was hanging a USED ADULT BOOKS sign in the window of a secondhand clothing and antique shop. She made a couple of leveling adjustments, stepped back, cocked her head to one side, then went off, leaving it hanging crooked. My first thought was to yell to her — yell, above all of this, yell: "It's still out of kilter, my dear!" — then, more realistically, I considered phoning the shop. But the phone was in the bedroom trapped with Eleanor. And if I did call, the woman might think I spent my time watching her every move from my perch and decide to call the police. Or she might get self-conscious, paranoid, and quit her job, or have a breakdown. And what if the crooked sign is only an advertising gimmick to attract attention, like the upside down ads in the classifieds, or the spastically-posed mannequins. She might say thanks for telling her, but she'd think, *Gotcha, you old fart*, and set every sign in the place askew.

Wendell forged ahead. "But the thing about depression...

the thing which separates the cured from the cursed is simply an understanding of the strategy of the ailment. Once you have depression's plan of attack, there you go."

He'd worked his way over to where I was sitting and was presently shampooing where my feet would have been if I hadn't raised them onto the windowsill. His silver mass lunged.

"Depression has to be on top of you to depress," he said. "If you're above it, then it's below you. It's push, therefore, can only lift. Am I right? You follow? I'm saying you can de*press* depression."

He raised his eyebrows ceilingward and started whistling along with the muffled siren of his tool, creating spiraling crescendos and decrescendos.

"Now there are entire bookcases full of methods for helping a person rise above depression, but they're all temporary fixes. And I wouldn't expect many of them to lift something like, say, involutional melancholia — but you don't look the involutional melancholic type."

Right when I thought he was going to talk me out the window, he veered off toward the kitchen. A curious melody and argument lifted from the street and tested the air where he'd been standing.

"There *is*, however, no denying you're gumption's been gunnysacked," he said, disappearing around the side of the refrigerator.

It felt better just having him out of sight.

"That's how Pastor G.D. would put it," he added.

"Don't you worry yourself about me," I said.

"I cannot help but."

"I'm fine as a fighting cock."

"You look kind of washed-out to these eyes," he said, still out of sight.

"Never felt better."

"Well, that's a syndrome too." He emerged. "In many cultures you would be a revered member of your community.

In some you'd be a national treaure. You, a national treasure. Think about that for a minute. I for one sympathize totally with the plight of the senior citizen in our western society. Neglected, ignored, forgotten, flushed. Nobody can blame you for feeling the way you do. I say something should be done about this whole state of affairs, and I say soon, don't you think?"

My joints ached. My lungs turned to wet flannel.

"Just how old *are* you, anyway?" asked Wendell.

Thrice the age of a dog is that of a horse;
Thrice the age of a horse is that of a man;
Thrice the age of a man is that of a deer;
Thrice the age of a deer is that of an eagle.

Thrice thrice thrice thrice, that's how the Celts of auld figured it. Thrice, three, the perfect number: beginning, middle, and end. I have definitely entered my thirdness.

"I'll tell you how old you are. You have reached the golden age of enlightened reason. At least you have the capacity for entering this phase of life — if only you can shed this earthly depression. Am I making sense to you?"

He headed my direction again, fixing his look squarely upon me. I shifted myself around to face outside. There is no one home, I meant him to understand.

Down on Grant, a skinny Italian man was cursing and making a gesture something like the one football referees use to indicate face-masking penalties. His taxi had just been stolen. The guy summoned a chase cab and off they went in dangerous pursuit through morning traffic, the young Italian slapping the side of the car like a whipless jockey.

"Some guy just stole a taxi," I said, more to myself than to Wendell. I leaned further out the window to watch the action. Both cars went screaming around the corner at St. Blandina, narrowly missing assorted collisions, then vanished.

Wendell's head was beside mine. He smelled of perfumed soap.

"Our own little city of thieves," he said. "But don't you worry at all: 'Stolen sustenance shall not nourish them. Their plates shall be filled with poisoned meats and their empires lost in their own widows' weeds.'"

"Widows' weeds," I said softly.

"You can credit that one to Pastor G.D. too. What a gift. What a vision."

His machine whined on as he returned to finish the kitchen.

I stepped down from the windowsill and gripped my bare toes into the wet carpet. By carefully disentangling select pieces of furniture and rearranging them, I was able to squirm through the puzzle, down the hallway — on my stomach, back, knees, in a crouch, waiting for the complete buggered trap to collapse — until I was hanging over one arm of the love seat, my head thrust between the legs of the coffee table, my fingertips just reaching the bedroom door.

"Eleanor?" I said, my face pushed into the cushioned back of the love seat. "Eleanor? Are you all right?"

I listened.

"Eleanor? Say something."

"You won't believe this. This is incredible," beamed big Wendell, two rooms away. "Last Sunday, Brother Horton called every last member of our church before service and set it up to where, when Pastor G.D. stood to deliver the principal sermon, the whole congregation rose on cue and did their best Cary Grant imitations. You should have heard all three hundred of us chanting away, 'G.D., G.D., G.D.' It was during our televised service. You didn't happen to catch it, did you?"

"Eleanor?"

"That's a true shame. It was plain incredible."

Hum to me Eleanor. Hum. Hum that soothing old-woman's hum of yours. That hum swelling up from your diaphragm, trilling in your breast. Eleanor? Hum. Almost a childlike hum, toying with pitch, timbre, and tempo. Filled with familiar but elusive phrases. Bits of nursery rhymes. *All the king's horses went to the cupboard to find the lost sheep*.

"Pastor G.D. laughed so hard his microphone squealed."

He was pulling my leg.

"I'll be damned," I said, trying to jerk my knee enough to pull loose.

"I refuse to believe that," he said. "You know, it was at the very same service that G.D. spoke so fiercely about the raw deal being given our retireds. 'We must lend our voice to the silenced seniors,' he said. 'For they are rich with God's wealth of wisdom. They shall know welcome in his divine employ. Let their worth be magnified in his ageless workforce.' Let me help you out of there."

I allowed myself to be extricated.

He'd finished his three rooms and shut off the shampooer, but the whirr seemed to continue, only slightly less deafening, as if the waves had a perpetual form and would forever haunt us. Wendell snapped the plug from the wall socket with a brisk yank on the cord and began winding it around his fist.

"I'd like you to meet G.D.," he said firmly.

"Of course," I said.

"He can explain much more convincingly than I how to make your retirement a fruitful and memorable time. There's no reason whatsoever for you to spend these years feeling depressed and alone. We can plug you into all kinds of worthwhile activities.

In Wendell's pulling, my pajama bottoms had somehow been twisted and were hanging half-off one hip. He smiled and straightened things for me.

"Do you really have this prime time to waste?" he asked. "Let me share something with you before I leave."

He grasped me by the shoulders and I watched his eyes tear. Outside, the horns seemed to agree on a common riff.

"I was driving over here to work this building this morning, right?" he began. "And this was fairly early because I commute in from Morton Hill and I go speed limit."

I nodded.

"It was maybe six-thirty, maybe earlier. There wasn't a soul on the streets. Now visualize this if you can: this city was like a modern ghost town. It was like I was the only man left on the planet. Can you see it? The only man left behind. It was like The Rapture. It was like everyone had departed without me. I quote to you from *I Thessalonians 4:16, 17*: 'For the Lord Himself shall descend from heaven with a shout, with the voice of the archangel, with the trumpet of God. And the dead in Christ shall rise first; then we who are alive and remain shall be caught up together with them in the clouds to meet the Lord in the air.' It was like I hadn't heard the shout, or the voice, or the trumpet, so I had been left behind on this sinful earth, to Tribulation."

He dug his thumbs in deeper.

"I was sweating plenty," he continued. "And I could hardly feel my legs — you know that feeling. So I stopped the van right there in the middle of my lane — I mean, who was going to hit me, right? I parked there and prayed for a good five minutes. Then I was taken by the urge to turn my radio on. Like in the gospel song, 'Turn it on, turn it on, turn your radio on.' And I did, I turned it on. But there was nothing at all. Dead silence. You can see precisely how this confirmed my fears."

"Yes," I said.

"I wept," Wendell said. "I sat back and wept, and I wondered where I'd stepped from the righteous path, which had been the wrong fork in my mortal journey. Then, about sixty seconds later, I heard Pastor G.D.'s voice speaking to me. 'That concludes our quiet time for this hour,' he said."

He released me with a quick slap on the back.

"Just you be ready is all I'm saying," said Wendell, hauling his machine toward the front door. He paused halfway out and said, "Elvin'll be by tomorrow."

I thought I heard my coccyx moan.

"You two will have a lot to talk about."

"Maybe so," I said.

"Elvin's a member of our Seniors' Crusade. He was also a close friend of my uncle's. He'll help you prepare to meet G.D."

And he was gone.

I went to the window and watched him come out of the building's main doors and climb into an old white van with a long, thick antenna sprouting from the roof. Traffic was still heavy with working people. Good jobs, bad jobs, joe jobs, snow jobs.

I pulled the window shut and began dragging furniture out of the hallway, sliding across the damp carpet. I would take Eleanor out for brunch, and we wouldn't return to the apartment until the damp dried and the noise waned. I wanted to hear only birds. Meadowlarks. I wanted to buy back our house.

"Oh, Eleanor," I complained as I finally flung open our bedroom door. I wanted to be hushed and mothered. Hummed to. I wanted to be rubbed where it ached. I wanted her to cut up laughing at this monstrous silver man, exorcise him from these rooms. "Oh, Eleanor," I said again, and started to drop beside her on the bed.

But she wasn't there.

I patted her side of the bed. I ran my palm over the rumpled sheets. She was not in the room.

I looked deeply into the dressing table mirror, as if she might've been lured through it into another dimension.

The bedroom curtains flapped at me, and I went to the window and leaned out, expecting to see her rising up through the city's air with thousands of other pure beings.

She reached up to me from her seat on the fire escape, took my hand and gave it a squeeze, my sweet hummer did, humming faintly, bless her, "Onward Christian Soldiers."